Eagle River Detectives, Book Three

Hide and Seek

Katherine H. Klemp

Eagle River Detectives, Book Three
Hide and Seek

by

Katherine H. Klemp

Copyright © 2023

Printed in the United States of America

ISBN: 979-8-9857710-3-9

First Edition
Independently Published

All rights reserved. This is a work of fiction. All the characters in this book are fictitious and the creation of the author's imagination. Any resemblance to persons living or dead is purely coincidental. No part of this publication may be reproduced or transmitted in any form or by any means, electronic or mechanical, including photocopy, recording, or any information storage retrieval system, without permission in writing from the copyright owner.

To my sisters:

*Paula Stansell,
Mary Hussmann,
Martha Bickel,
and Elizabeth Hussmann Hooi,*

*all of whom have had a lifelong
love affair with books.*

*Special thanks to my
granddaughters, Emily Klemp and
Isabelle Berwald and Isabelle's
other grandma, my friend, Cathy
Berwald, for the illustrations.*

This book has a free collection of activity sheets.
To get the FREE activity booklet end an email to:
katherineklemp@gmail.com or sign up at:
www.katherineklemp.com
and use the drop-down menu to find your bundle.

Learn more about the Eagle River Detectives by going to:
katherineklemp.com

To learn more about the author go to:
Facebook.com/katherineklempbooks

Contents

Prologue - Did That Really Happen? 1
1 – New Kids 3
2 – I Like This Guy 7
3 – Did That Really Happen? 12
4 – Summer Sets In 16
5 – Who Were Those Guys? 22
6 – No Show 30
7 – Who Did This? 35
8 – The Eagle River Detectives Explained 40
9 – Something to Investigate 45
10 – New Revelations 50
11 – An Enlightening Mealtime 55
12 – A Day in the Woods 60
13 – The Map 66
14 – Tim and Gabby Make a Good Team 69
15 – The Real Map 76
16 – What's Next? 81
17 – Gramps, Dear Gramps 85
18 – Marco 91
19 – Sally's 96
20 – Larry Diller 101
21 – The Factory 107
22 – Finding Marco 114
23 – Marco Rocks! 121

24 – Gramps and Ernie	125
25 – A Talk with George Evans	133
26 – What Next?	138
27 – Chasing Down the Final Clue	142
28 – The Playhouse	149
29 – The Wrap-Up	153
Author's Note	155
About the Author	156

Prologue

Did That Really Happen?
June

Gabby and Jodie Grant sat side-by-side at a picnic table at Eagle Point, the city park at the edge of town. The twelve-year-old twins had ridden their bikes to the park to meet with their new friends, Owen and Vivian Sampson. Gabby and Jodie had lived in Eagle River, Nebraska, for two years now, but they well remembered how hard it had been to be the new kids at school in a small town where most of the other children had been going to school together since kindergarten.

Owen was in seventh grade with them, and Vivian was two years younger, in fifth grade. The two new kids had started school when there were only six weeks left before summer vacation. At the time, Gabby thought it would have been easier for the kids to fit in if they had just waited to start school at the beginning of next year, but their parents must have thought differently.

Now, here they were, at the beginning of a hot Nebraska summer, and things were getting weird. The twins didn't see any sign of their new friends, but they had been watching two men maneuvering a rowboat along the shore of the river. Because of the heavy brush, Gabby was pretty sure neither of the men had seen them yet. The twins sat as still as possible. Any movement could call attention to their presence.

Gabby could only hear an occasional word or two as the men spoke quietly to one another. "Where did…kids disappear to?"

Another voice muttered, "They…bikes."

"Keep looking…somewhere."

1

New Kids

(Earlier) April

"Jodie, let's go!" Gabby waited impatiently for his twin to grab her backpack and lunch. The two of them usually rode bikes to school, and while it wasn't raining yet, it felt like the downpour was not going to hold off much longer. Thunk! Jodie fell to the floor of the porch, her backpack flying out of her hand into the nearby bushes.

"Ball, you stupid dog!" The uninjured girl sprang to her feet as quickly as she had fallen, dug her pack out of the shrubbery, climbed on her bike, and glared at her laughing brother. "Well, are we going or not?"

This was not the first time Jodie had begun her day in this fashion. Everyone in the family knew that Ball's favorite spot was right in front of the door, but Jodie was usually in such a hurry that she forgot. Ball ran to Jodie, a ball in his mouth, totally pleased with himself. Gabby thought it hilarious that the dog went running to fetch a ball when anyone called his name.

Jodie was already halfway down the street by the time Gabby recovered from his laughing fit and came pedaling after her. The days were getting warmer and the buds on the trees were bursting into deep green leaves. It was full-on springtime, and the twins rode to school enjoying the colorful tulips and the bright yellow Forsythia blossoms in the trim front yards they passed. As they drew near to the school, they could tell something unusual was happening. Kids were drifting into small groups, and animated conversations were going on everywhere.

Gabby coasted up to a group of guys he knew. "What's the big excitement?" he asked Franklin, a pudgy kid in his gym class.

"We're getting some new students, and there is supposedly some mystery around their family moving here." Franklin was pleased to have a chance to spread the big news of the day. Eagle River was a town of about 1,200; a good size by Nebraska standards, but any change in the town's makeup made people take note. Eagle River was not a hive of innovation. Same old, same old was more this town's style.

Gabby knew that from experience. It hadn't taken long for him and his siblings to figure out that they were not welcome when they had first moved to town two years ago. The kids formed the Eagle River Detectives in order to find out why they were disliked. Gabby clearly remembered the dangerous and frustrating months before they uncovered the problem and won the town over to their side.

"What did Franklin have to say?" Jodie asked her twin.

"He said there were new kids coming to school and there was some mystery around their moving here," Gabby reported.

"Maybe we should meet these kids and uncover the family secret," Jodie kidded. "After all, we are detectives, aren't we?"

Finding out why they hadn't been welcomed by the town wasn't the only case they had solved since moving to Eagle River. Earlier this year, they had helped their brother, Tim, solve the mystery of his girlfriend's missing uncle. That had proved more dangerous and more involved than they had realized at the time. "But," Jodie had reminded the group, "it's a good thing we didn't give up. A lot of people would have gotten hurt if we hadn't kept going."

The twins were in seventh grade, and the talk in the halls was that one of the new kids was a seventh grader, too. Gabby's first class of the day was social studies. No new kid showed up during that class. Jodie had no new student to report from her math class when she and Gabby met in the hall. The next class for both of them was science with Ms. Sanders. Shortly before the class started, the principal entered the room with a skinny, brown-haired, brown skinned, boy in tow. Jodie whispered to Gabby that the newcomer could use a haircut, but that she really liked his big brown eyes.

"Class, I'd like to introduce this young man to you all," Mr. Hooper explained. "His name is Owen Sampson, and I expect you to make sure he feels welcome at Eagle River Junior High."

Owen Sampson gave a nod to the kids and waited for whatever came next. Ms. Sanders smiled at the boy and showed him where to sit. His desk was right next to Gabby's, so Gabby stood and shook the new boy's hand in welcome. The newcomer's shoulders seemed to relax a bit, and he gave Gabby a grateful smile.

"Owen, could you stand up and tell us a little about yourself? We'd like to get to know you." Ms. Sanders addressed the newcomer. Owen looked mortified at the request.

Gabby gave him a look of sympathy. Nobody enjoyed being put on the spot like that, especially in seventh grade.

Owen stood up as asked, but he looked only at Ms. Sanders, purposefully avoiding looking at the kids in the class. "What do you want to know?"

"Why don't you start with where you come from," the teacher said with an encouraging smile.

"Well, I really couldn't say, but thanks for asking." At that Owen sat down and didn't say another word.

2

I Like This Guy

Gabby couldn't get over the masterful way Owen had ended the interchange with Ms. Sanders. When he sat down, the teacher looked at the newcomer with surprise, shrugged and turned to the lesson for the day. Gabby loved conversation and words—and communication in general. He was pretty sure that he and Owen were going to hit it off. He didn't run into the new kid the rest of the school day, so he went looking for him after school.

"Hey, Jodie," he hailed his sister. She was standing next to her bike, talking with the very person he was looking for. Both heads turned his way at his greeting. Owen's eyes lighted up.

"Gabby, is it?" the boy said. "I really want to thank you for making that new kid thing a lot easier. It meant a lot to me to feel like I might have a friend in the room."

"I thought you managed the 'tell us about yourself' episode with real class," Gabby grinned.

"Nice of you to say so," Owen acknowledged the compliment. "I've found that the least said the better."

"That is definitely something that you've not discovered yet," Jodie teased her twin.

A pig-tailed girl in a yellow tee and a blue jean skirt joined the group. "I've been looking for you everywhere," she said to Owen. "I thought you left me here to rot."

"You would have to die first, and then it would take another week or two before your body would begin to decay," Owen responded. "You don't look dead to me." He playfully tugged one of the girl's dark pigtails. "This is my sister, Vivian. Don't pay any attention to her. She's spoiled enough already."

Gabby liked the playful way the new siblings treated one another. "Hi, Vivian. I'm Gabby and this is my spoiled sister, Jodie. You two should get along just fine."

Vivian went over to Jodie and gave her a high-five. "Spoiled sisters rule," she exclaimed. That had the whole group laughing.

* * *

"We need to get to know those two better. I liked them both," said Jodie as she and Gabby pedaled home.

Home was a large two-story house about six blocks from school. Gabby and his siblings had moved to Eagle River two years ago to live in the large house with Grandpa Bertram, while their mom was working outside the country. Dad had died a couple of years earlier, and they were a sad little group when they had first moved to town. Besides his twin sister, he had an older sister, Carly, who was a junior in high school, and a brother, Tim, who was a first-year student at Eagle River High.

The kids had grown to love the town. Gramps had moved out of the big house so that his daughter, Julie, her the kids, and her new husband, Papa John, could enjoy the spacious home in which she had grown up. Gramps was happy to move into an assisted living facility called Sumner Place. He already knew most of the residents, because he had lived in Eagle River all his life.

Gabby's stepdad, Papa John, was a lawyer, and one of Mom's childhood friends. Gabby was pleased that Papa John was a big support when his mom took on the ambitious project of getting the Grant Manufacturing plant up and running again. The kids were delighted when they discovered the ownership had fallen to Mom after Grandpa Grant and Dad had died. The town was grateful for the economic boost of having both old and new jobs available to them. The furniture made at the plant had a reputation for excellence all across the Midwest. Tim, who was only fourteen, had inherited the family business gene, and couldn't wait to take over the plant when he was old enough. He once told Gabby, "I'm going to make Grant furniture known across the whole country someday."

Right on que, Ball came running down the porch steps to greet the bikers. As usual, he wound between the children's bikes, making it difficult to turn into the yard. Gabby was the first to make a safe stop. He grabbed Ball's collar to keep Jodie from tipping over. In addition to being the welcome committee, the dog had the reputation of being a wrecking "ball." He simply charged into the middle of whatever the children were doing.

Having safely navigated the big furball's attack, Gabby led the way to the kitchen. The kitchen was where the family met most often. The large table in the center of the room was inviting. They all led busy lives, but mealtime, especially in the evening, was considered important, and rarely did anyone miss supper. Carly was spreading a ketchup and brown sugar mixture on top of her meatloaf before putting it in the oven. She had taken over the cooking responsibilities so that Mom could concentrate on the factory.

"There are cookies in the cookie jar, but no more than two," she told the twins. "Supper will be ready before you know it." Gabby, who was at that stage where he was hungry all the time, gratefully grabbed two cookies and plopped down on one of the kitchen chairs.

"We might have a new case developing," he told his big sister, watching her reaction out of the corner of his eye. Carly continued her preparations for the evening meal. "There's a family that moved into town. Rumor has it, that there is some mystery around their coming here," he continued. "Jodie thinks it's worth looking into."

At that, Carly turned toward her little brother and rolled her eyes. "Gabby, I know you loved being a part of our last two cases. The first one cleared up Dad's name, and in the second we helped find Olivia's uncle. I know we saved the town from a serious disaster, but we didn't go looking for those adventures. We just stepped in where we were needed. Don't try to manufacture a new case."

Tim had entered the kitchen in time to hear the whole exchange. "Carly's right, you know. With Dad, it involved us, and Olivia's mom *asked* us to help with Roberto. Detectives don't snoop into other people's business without a good reason."

Gabby respected his older siblings and could see their point. "Well, we met the two kids in school today and liked them both a lot. I guess if there is any way the Eagle River Detectives can be of service, they will let us know."

3

Did That Really Happen?

Over the next six weeks of school, the more Gabby got to know Owen, the closer the boys became. Both played on the school's baseball team, and both loved to fish. Jodie and Vivian hit it off as well, and now that school was over, they had lots of plans for the summer break.

Gabby was up and dressed on Tuesday morning, waiting for Jodie to come down for breakfast.

"Why are you up so early?" Carly asked. "I thought you would be sleeping in now that school is out."

"Are you kidding?" Jodie joined the conversation, practically leaping down the stairs. "This is the best time of the year, and we don't want to miss a moment of it. We're going fishing with Owen and Vivian."

The twins ate quickly and said goodbye to Carly. Grabbing their poles and gear, they headed for the park. Eagle River was a small town, and nothing was too far away. The park was maybe ten blocks from their house at the edge of town. The streets were wide and level, and a good bike could get you pretty much anywhere you wanted to go.

They were the first ones to arrive, so they found a seat on the picnic table. It was a beautiful, sunny morning, and they were content to watch the river flow past as they waited for their friends.

"I'm surprised they aren't here by now. They always seemed to get to school earlier than we did." Gabby was getting a little worried.

The twins sat silently. They didn't see any sign of their friends, but they did watch two men maneuvering a rowboat along the shore of the river. There was heavy brush edging the riverbank, so Gabby was sure neither of the men had seen them yet, but the two men were watching something. The twins intuitively sat as still as possible. The slightest movement could call attention to their presence.

Gabby could only hear an occasional word or two as the men spoke quietly to one another. "Where did…kids disappear to?"

Another voice muttered, "They…bikes."

"Keep looking…somewhere."

Just then, two cars pulled into the parking area. A half-dozen teens spilled out into the park. Laughing and shoving and showing off for one another, they headed for the path along the riverbank. If they saw the men in the boat, they paid no attention. Their cheerful voices echoed across the water.

The men, however, apparently wanted nothing to do with the new arrivals. They quickly turned the boat around and rowed to the opposite shore from which they had come.

A flustered Jodie faced her twin. "Do we wait, or do we get out of here right now?"

Once the men were fully out of sight, Gabby motioned Jodie to follow him to the path along the river. "Those men were looking along the bank about here. It sounded like they had seen someone at some point and then lost sight of them."

"Owen? Vivian?" Jodie called their friends' names in a voice just above a whisper. She was well aware that sound carried across water.

Vivian's head appeared, cautiously scanning the area.

"Are they gone?" she asked in a low voice. "That was a close call."

Owen appeared next, pulling his bike out of the river where it had been submerged. Gabby waded into the water to help Vivian pull her bike out of the weedy river's edge.

"What was that about? Who were those men? Why were they looking for you?" Gabby riddled the pair with questions.

Owen, his clothes wet and muddy and his hair plastered to his head, looked at his agitated friend and then looked away. "Well, I really couldn't say. But thanks for asking."

Gabby looked at Jodie questioningly. Should he let Owen get by with his lame response? What had seemed like a clever answer when Owen was responding to Ms. Sanders at school a few weeks ago, seemed a lot like evasion now.

Gabby helped Vivian get her bike up the bank and on to firm ground. "I'll let that answer slide for now," he told Owen. "But if we are to be real friends, the next time I ask that question, you need to have a better answer than that."

Owen looked Gabby in the eye and nodded. Gabby wasn't sure what that nod meant. It could've gone either way.

4

Summer Sets In

Owen and Vivian climbed on their bikes, and without another word, left the park. Gabby and Jodie rehashed that morning's events over and over, even to the following day. "Have you ever heard of kids who have adults chasing them? Who were those guys?" Jodie was upset just thinking about yesterday.

"Why didn't they explain any of it to us? Surely, they knew we would try to help." Gabby slathered mayo on a ham and cheese sandwich for his lunch. He and Jodie intended to go to the park again, just the two of them this time. He was hurt that their new friends didn't trust them. *If we are even friends anymore.* "I don't know what to do now," he said, sighing.

"Well, the ball's in their court." Jodie liked using sayings she picked up from Carly. She had to ask what that one meant when she first heard it, though. Gabby had heard Carly explain that it was like a tennis match. If the ball was on the other player's side of the net, you couldn't continue

Summer Sets In

the game until they hit it back to your side. They would have to wait until Owen or Vivian made the next move.

Tim came down the stairs three or four at a time. He had a job at the hardware store in town and was working there about six hours most days. Gabby missed having his big brother join in their jaunts to the park. Ball was coming with them today, and Tim loved playing frisbee while Ball made a nuisance of himself with the players. He claimed that having Ball run around and chase the kids gave the game a little extra spice. Trying to catch the disk without tripping on the dog was the real challenge.

"Hey, Gabby," Tim called. "Don't you have a new kid in your class this year?"

"You mean Owen?" Gabby asked. "What about him?"

"Well, he knew that in Nebraska you could get a driver's license at age fifteen, but he wanted to know how old you had to be to get a hunting license and a gun."

* * *

Ball loped alongside the children's bikes, happy to be invited along. Gabby was deep in thought. He, Jodie, Tim, and perhaps Carly would be going to Sumner House later that afternoon to visit Gramps. Gabby looked forward to that visit for two reasons: Gramps and Ernie. Ernie was a retired police officer turned retired detective who got a big kick out of the Eagle River Detectives. Ernie had never married, so Gramps generously shared his grandkids with his friend. Gabby was the detective's favorite.

"Do you think we should ask Ernie what he thinks about those guys looking for Owen and Vivian?" Gabby asked his twin.

"We don't really know if it was Owen and Vivian they were looking for, and until those two confide in us, it's none of our business. Besides, maybe just asking the question would call too much attention to them. They didn't want to tell us anything, so whatever is going on is something they want to keep to themselves." Jodie was observant and sensitive to other people's situations.

Gabby reluctantly agreed. They needed to move on. The twins had decided that their goal for the summer was to create a code that they could use just between the Eagle River Detective club members. Gabby had listened to some online videos about people who had secret signals, secret handshakes, and secret codes. They were going to work on the code project at one of the picnic tables at the park.

Once they were seated, Gabby pulled a notebook out of his backpack and opened to a blank page. He then wrote out the alphabet, leaving a lot of space between the letters. "Any code needs a starting place, and the alphabet is a good place to start for our purposes. We all know the alphabet by heart, so we will be able to solve the code from anywhere, as long as we know the key."

"What's a key?" Jodie was sure her twin was not talking about a real key, the kind you used to open a locked door.

"Well, when things are written in a coded language, there is a secret way to "unlock" the message, and the secret is called the key. Both the person who writes the message and the person who "unlocks" the message use the same secret trick. A simple code would be to turn the alphabet around, and the key to the trick would be that instead of using an A in your message you would use a Z to mean A." Gabby looked at Jodie, checking to see if she understood.

"Huh? Remind me again." Jodie didn't get it at first.

"Look." Gabby was patient with his twin. He took his pencil and began to write other letters underneath those he had already put into the book:

A B C D E F G H I J K L M N O P Q R S T U V W X Y Z
Z Y X W V U T S R Q P O N M L K J I H G F E D C B A

"The key to the message is to use the letter below to mean the one above."

"So, if I want to spell my name, I start with the top letter, but then use the secret letter below. J becomes Q, because Q is below J. O is now L, D is W, I is R, and E is V. Qlwrv. *Jodie* in code!"

"Then if I knew the key," Gabby explained, "I could take your secret name, Qlwrv, and change it back to the real letters on top, and it would spell out Jodie." Gabby was pleased at how quickly his sister caught on. Jodie was a smart one.

"Brilliant!" Jodie praised her twin.

HVV RU BLF XZM IVZW GSRH. Gabby handed her a slip of paper with a coded message. "Now that you know the key, what does this say?"

Jodie borrowed Gabby's pencil and went to work. It didn't take her long. "The message says, 'See if you can read this', and the answer is, 'BYH R XZM.'"

"Fascinating," said a sudden voice from behind.

Gabby turned to see Owen peering at the notebook, his eyes widening in delight at the cypher.

"Yes, I can," Owen translated Jodie's answer.

"That's impressive," Vivian chimed in. The two new kids had parked their bikes and were standing by the picnic table. Gabby and Jodie had been so wrapped up in their project they hadn't seen the others enter the park. Ball was sitting next to the two, looking expectantly at the twins.

Vivian gave Owen a stern look. "We came to apologize," Owen said reluctantly, shoving his hands into his pockets.

Vivian gave him a look of approval and added, "Owen and I have had to move around a lot in these past few years, and every time we change schools, it gets harder and harder to find friends. That's why we felt bad for what we did yesterday."

Ball watched Vivian as she talked, then turned to Owen when he spoke up.

Owen looked to the ground. "It's especially hard when we are in a town where there are not many other Black families. We get a little defensive, I guess. It's hard when people judge you by the color of your skin."

"Well, if it's any consolation, when we moved to Eagle River, people judged us by our last name, and they didn't particularly like us because of it." Gabby was thinking back to some of the unkind comments people made to them when they were new in town. At the time, they had no idea why. "Anyway, apology accepted."

Jodie went over and gave Vivian a friendly hug, and Gabby gave Owen a slap on the back. Ball ran off to explore the park, satisfied that all was well.

"Maybe you can help us refine our secret code," Jodie was already back to the task at hand.

"Why do you need a secret code?" Vivian climbed over the seat and sat by Jodie.

"It seems like something detectives might need if they want to communicate without others knowing when they figure stuff out," Jodie countered.

"So, are you planning to become detectives when you grow up? That's hilarious. You could call yourselves Twin Sleuths, Inc." Owen enjoyed teasing people.

"We don't have to wait until we grow up," Gabby said, exchanging a knowing look with Jodie.

5

Who Were Those Guys?

"We haven't forgotten, you know." Gabby stood in front of Owen, hands on hips. "You promised to explain about those men who were chasing you." Jodie and Vivian stopped what they were doing. Ball had returned to sit by the picnic table. All eyes were on Owen.

"Oh, that." Owen shrugged. "They weren't exactly chasing us; they were just checking up on us."

"Then why did you hide?" Jodie wasn't buying it. Those men had been coming after the kids; he was sure of it. If those teenagers hadn't spilled out of their cars at just the right moment, they would not have given up so easily.

Vivian got up and went to stand by her brother. "He's telling the truth. They show up every time we move to a new town, but they never hurt us or anything. They just want to ask us questions about where we are living now, why we are in this town, and stuff like that. We don't think it is any of their business, so we try to hide until they give up and go away."

"What do they want?" Gabby was struggling with the information that this was not the first time the kids had hidden from these men.

Owen shrugged again. "We're not sure, but we think they want something from our mom. That's why we don't like it when they ask their questions."

"They turn up whenever we move, so someone close to us has to be watching us, too. How else would they find out so quickly?" Vivian added.

Gabby detected a quaver in her voice as she spoke. She tried not to show it, but he could tell; she was a little scared.

"Did you pack a lunch like we did?" Jodie, noticing that both Owen and Vivian were carrying backpacks, had decided it was time to change the subject.

"Owen never forgets food," Vivian teased her brother. Owen was in the same stage as Gabby: growing boy, always hungry.

The kids unpacked their lunches. Gabby pulled out a bowl for Ball and emptied a bottle of water into it. It was a hot day, and Ball lapped eagerly. After he emptied the bowl, he found some nearby shade and stretched out for a nap. There was a faint breeze, but not enough to rattle the leaves. An occasional bee buzzed by, going from flower bed to flower bed.

As they enjoyed their food, Owen shared that he was keen to learn how to hunt. He said he grew up on stories of his dad hunting pheasant and wild turkeys. This was the first time they lived in a small town where people still did things like hunting and fishing. He hoped that when his dad came back from a tour of duty overseas the two of them could go hunting together. Vivian was an avid reader, and she and Jodie traded titles of the books they had read recently.

"Every Wednesday the bookmobile comes to the park," Jodie told her new friend. "That's tomorrow, so we can get you a library card then if you don't already have one." Vivian was delighted.

"Don't forget your fishing poles tomorrow. We can get in plenty of fishing before your dad gets home," Gabby reminded their new friends. He and Jodie both liked to fish, and Eagle River ran right through the park.

After a leisurely lunch, the four friends walked slowly to their bikes and began pedaling toward the park entrance. They could hear screams of delight coming from the kids at the swimming pool at the top of the hill. They rode lazily past the playground equipment where moms watched carefully as their little ones played. Five boys were having a shooting contest on the basketball court. It was summer—time for relaxation and fun, not worry about strange men trying to get information out of a couple of kids.

Jodie returned to the morning's events. "We need to get to the bottom of this. There has to be a logical explanation. Does your mom know about these guys?" Jodie hoped Vivian and Owen weren't trying to deal with this on their own.

"She knows," Owen explained. "She says that as far as she is concerned, they are barking up the wrong tree. Whatever it is they want from her, she doesn't have it. She tells us not to worry and says we can tell them whatever they want to know, since there is nothing for them to find out."

"Maybe your mom knows something she doesn't know she knows," Gabby offered.

Owen started laughing. "How can she know something she doesn't know?"

"Like Gabby said, she doesn't know she knows. It might be something she knows, but doesn't think is important, so she never thinks about it." Jodie tried to explain what Gabby was trying to say. They were nearly home.

Gabby noticed that Ball was loping along behind the bikes like a normal dog, which was not normal for Ball. Just before they turned into the driveway, Ball picked up speed and wove in and out of the four bikes creating chaos for the riders. Gabby grabbed on to Vivian's handlebars so that she would not fall over, and Jodie just managed to hop off her bike before she crashed into the porch.

Oh, good. Gabby was beginning to worry that Ball was sick or something.

* * *

The four kids agreed to meet at the park again in the morning. Owen and Vivian pedaled off, and Gabby guessed by their happy banter, they were as pleased as the twins were to have found new summer friends.

They found Carly in the kitchen. She was putting a large pan of lasagna into the refrigerator. "I've got supper ready to pop into the oven, so, as long as we can be home by 4:30,

I can come with you to see Gramps. Tim is home already, so he's coming too.

"What about Michael?" Gabby was asking about Carly's boyfriend. He often came with them on their weekly visit. Michael was a frequent visitor to the Grant home and had officially become an Eagle River Detective on their last case. Gabby thought of him as almost a member of the family.

"He's putting in some extra hours at the plant today," Carly answered as she took off her apron and combed her hair.

Michael was a genius at furniture design. Gramps had seen something of himself in the young boy and had helped him develop his talent. Gramps had been an expert designer in his day, and his designs had helped Grant Manufacturing become famous for their furniture. Now Mom had hired Michael to collaborate with the current designers. Gabby knew that Tim was a little jealous that Michael already worked at the plant. Tim had inherited his father's and grandfather's business sense and loved Grant Manufacturing. Mom had promised him a job when he turned sixteen; Tim would only turn fifteen this summer, so Gabby wasn't surprised at his impatience.

The siblings climbed into Carly's car. The family had gotten a new van, so Carly was buying the car from Mom. It gave the kids a lot more freedom, and Michael made sure to keep it well cared for.

"What were you two up to today?" Tim asked the twins as he scrolled through his phone. Tim's blond hair was sticking up in back. He was wearing a Nike t-shirt that had seen better days. It was starting to pull a little tightly to his growing chest, and his voice seemed to have dropped an octave since summer started. Gabby barely recognized this Tim from the one who started high school last year.

"We had a very interesting morning," Jodie piped up. "We have a cool code to show you. It's going to be great for sending secret messages."

Tim looked up from his phone, turned and looked at the twins in the back seat, shook his head in amazement, and muttered to Carly, "What will they think up next?"

* * *

Sumner House was a two-story brick building with a pleasant archway over the large front door. The kids ignored the front entrance and instead scooted around back where there was a lovely pavilion that supplied a shady place to sit. Both Gramps and Ernie were there, enjoying the colorful flowers and the pleasant sound of the fountain in the center of the garden-like backyard.

Gabby gave Gramps a big hug, and then did the same for Ernie. Both men teared up a little as the kids each filed by for their hugs. There were plenty of chairs, so the kids set their seats to form a circle so everyone could talk. This was one of Gabby's favorite activities for the week.

"What's the news for the detective business?" Ernie asked the same question every week. He got a big kick out of their sleuthing. He used to ask that question to tease them a little. Over the last two cases, though, he had grown to respect their abilities. These kids were the real deal.

Gabby was always the first to speak. "I don't know if it is detective news, but we have become good friends with the two new kids in town."

"How are the kids at school treating them? It can't be easy for them." Gramps and Ernie knew about Owen and Vivian from when they had first come to town. Gramps even remembered that there was another time that a Black family had lived in Eagle River. He had told the kids that the father of that family had worked for Grandpa Grant. The people in town hadn't had a problem accepting that family because many of the townspeople also worked at Grant Manufacturing and had gotten to know Albert Decker personally. Gramps said he was a real character. "He was a smart guy, too," Gramps had added.

"I think they are doing fine," Jodie said. "Vivian is a funny jokester, and Owen is very friendly. They seem to fit right in."

Carly told Gramps about one of Michael's ideas for a coffee table, and Tim reported that his job at the hardware store was getting more and more interesting as he got to know more about the merchandise. Gramps asked about his daughter, their mom, and Gabby told a funny story about Mom and Ball.

The air became cooler as some clouds moved in. It was supposed to rain that night. It was a pleasant visit, and the kids gave the men goodbye hugs, and headed back to the car.

"Same old, same old," Gabby said with a sigh. He wished they had a case to report on.

"Same old, same old," Tim agreed, sighing in relief. He had had enough excitement with the last two cases.

Nobody who saw that little gathering would ever guess the crazy way the summer would turn out.

6

No Show

Gabby and Jodie had been fishing for a whole hour, and there was still no sign of their friends. The twins had left Ball home and were glad they did. There were three kids tossing a frisbee around, and that would have been chaos if Ball was there. They had pretty well exhausted their ideas on why Owen and Vivian were not at the park as planned: they had forgotten, they had found something better to do, they secretly found the twins boring, they had moved to another town, they were actually afraid of those men following them.

Gabby cast expertly into the flowing river, but once again reeled back in without a single nibble. "Well, they didn't miss much as far as catching fish is concerned," he muttered. Both kids were disappointed. They had come to the park excited to learn more about their new friends.

"I just don't get it." Jodie, tired of the tedious task of not catching fish, had already retired her pole. She sat on the riverbank watching the ever-hopeful Gabby continue to fish. "I can't tell if it means that they don't like us, or if there is a deeper mystery here."

Just then the mobile library truck pulled into the parking area and set up shop. Gabby could tell that made Jodie even sadder. She had been excited to show her new friend some of her favorite books.

"Let's just go." Gabby reeled in his line, closed the tackle box, and retrieved his bike.

The twins rolled lazily out of the park and down the street toward home. The leafy trees on either side gave enough shade to blunt the heat of the sun. Summer was Gabby's favorite time of the year, and he wasn't going to let a little disappointment ruin this glorious day.

Carly had left a salad in the refrigerator for anyone seeking lunch. Gabby got out bread and ham slices for sandwiches. Tim came flying into the room, grabbed the sandwich Gabby had just finished making, and flew just as quickly out the door. "Thanks, Gab," he mumbled, his mouth full of food. "I'm trying not to be late for work."

Gabby looked at his empty plate and the empty space that his brother had occupied moments earlier. "You're welcome," he said to the empty space. Gabby made himself another sandwich, and the twins ate in companiable silence.

"Let's go to the playhouse and work some more on our code." Jodie smiled at her brother. She could usually come up with good ideas to make the day fun. Carly had told Gabby once that Michael was continually amazed that the twins always seemed to be up to something that they enjoyed doing.

The playhouse was one of Jodie's favorite places in the whole world. Last fall, Mom had the small cabin that she and their father had played in as kids moved onto the Grant Manufacturing plant grounds. When the kids stumbled across it, it was a total surprise. They all loved the cozy cabin. They had already had some adventures because of it, but the twins hadn't been over there for almost a month.

The plant was about a mile and a half out of town, but that was within biking distance. The roads were flat and paved, and not busy most days. Gabby had brought his notebook and was thinking about new ways to make the code harder to break.

The cabin was as inviting as ever. Cute curtains showed on the windows, and the newly painted green shutters gave it a cared-for look. The kids parked their bikes and Gabby dug out the key. Jodie had rushed ahead of him and turned the door handle. Surprisingly, it moved freely in her hand.

"Oh, look, it's not locked," she said, turning her head to tell Gabby as she pushed open the door.

Gabby was the first to see it. The placed had been trashed!

* * *

Gabby and Jodie had at once gone to the main building of the plant. They found Mom in her office and brought her to view the damage. Gabby knew Tim was still at work, but he called Carly to let her know about the break-in. She needed to see this.

Mom stood in the middle of the mess, tears gathering in her eyes, hugging herself for comfort as she looked around at the jumbled mess. "How did they get on the property? Who would dare to do this to a children's playhouse? This is supposed to be a safe haven when children can be carefree and play. This is unacceptable." Mom was on a rant. "We are going to get to the bottom of this. Someone is going to find out that they messed with the wrong family." She stamped her foot in frustration.

Mom loved this cabin as much as the kids did. This place held so many memories of her childhood. Gramps and Grandfather Grant had had a great time building it for their kids. And their grandmothers had spent hours decorating the small cabin, sewing curtains, and furnishing the living room and kitchen. Gabby still had trouble picturing his mom and dad playing here as kids. Mom's rant was magnificent, though. Gabby could see where Carly got her grit.

Jodie went over to Mom seeking comfort. "What are we going to do?" The kitchen table and chairs were on their sides as though someone had flung them down in frustration. The kitchen drawers were pulled out and the contents dumped carelessly on the floor. The Murphy bed was pulled down from the living room wall with the mattress flung to the floor. Sheets and blankets had been pulled off the bed and were lying in a heap in the corner of the room. Ashes covered the hearth in front of the fireplace. All the couch cushions were askew, as though the intruders had searched for something in the frame.

"Well, honey, it's not so much the mess. We can put the place back together to look just like it did before this happened, but then we are going to find the intruders and make them wish they had left it alone." Gabby could tell Mom was still hopping mad. "Right now, the safety of my children is all that matters."

"Carly and Michael stepped through the door and viewed the mess. "I hate knowing that strangers were inside our playhouse touching our things and making a mess of the place. How did they get in here?" Carly asked her mom.

"We don't know yet," Mom told the new arrivals. "But we're going to find out."

7

Who Did This?

The topic at the supper table was, of course, the break-in. Who did it? Was it a random action? Was it someone they knew being mean? Would they try to do it again? By the end of the meal, they were no closer to any real answers. Now the whole family was back at the playhouse, determined to restore the beloved cabin to its original order.

"You were right, Mom. Things are going pretty well on the clean-up," Tim noted. "I mean, whoever did this didn't cause any real damage to the property."

Gabby looked around the room. He had just finished sweeping up the ashes in front of the fireplace. Mom and Carly had put the sheets, pillows, and bedspread back on the Murphy bed and had it folded neatly into its place up against the wall. Jodie had picked up most of the contents on the kitchen floor and had returned the items to the drawers they had come from. Papa John had the table and overturned chairs sorted neatly into place, and after Tim put the cushions and pillows back on the couch, the room looked pretty good.

"You mean they didn't actually destroy anything, right?" Jodie saw the transformation, too.

Gabby pictured the place as they first saw it, and then looked again at how it was already back to normal. "They didn't come here to mess the place up," he said. "They came here looking for something."

"I think you're right, Gabby." The place had been a mess, but, as Tim had pointed out, it looked more like it was searched rather than vandalized.

"That may be true, but the fact that they were in here at all is concerning. Why would anyone search a playhouse? You kids don't keep money here, do you?" Mom looked at the kids, scanning their faces for some clue.

"I can't think of anything anyone else would think was valuable. Can any of you?" Carly looked at her siblings. The others shook their heads, practically in unison. They truly had no idea of anything anyone would want that was kept there.

"From now on I am going to have one of our surveillance cameras mounted on the light pole near the playhouse, and I'll make sure the night watchman makes a check on the property at least once on his nightly rounds." Mom was taking no chances on this happening again.

"Good." Jodie smiled at Mom. Jodie loved that playhouse as much as her mother did.

"I don't think it will matter much," Gabby mused. "They didn't find what they were looking for, so I don't think they will be back." He looked at Tim as they were climbing into the car. "But, guess what, dear brother of mine. We have a new case!"

* * *

The following morning found the twins back at the park. The place was busier than normal, but they were able to capture an open picnic table and Gabby got out the notepad and pencils. Jodie thought that just reversing the letters might not make the code difficult enough. Someone might guess that the key when they saw the Z under the A and the A under the Z.

Gabby suggested taking out the vowels, A, E, I, O, U and sometimes Y and putting them at the end of the alphabet, so that the backwards words would be hard to read. Hold the A and start with B instead.

B C D F G H J K L M N P Q R S T V W X Z A E I O U Y
Z Y X W V U T S R Q P O N M L K J I H G F E D C B A

"That might work." Jodie agreed. "After all, Owen barely had time to look over your shoulder at the code and was able to decode the message easily."

"Well, that's because I'm smarter than average, aren't I, Vivian?" Once again Owen and Vivian were standing next to the picnic table, their bikes parked behind them. "I guess we owe you an apology." Owen searched Gabby's face worriedly.

Gabby could see the boy was unsure if he was going to be able to repair the damage to their friendship. "We're listening." Gabby knew he and Jodie had been more disappointed than angry when the two had not come as promised and was hoping they could still be friends.

"Well, when we got home after leaving you at your house, Mom was sitting on our front porch waiting for us. She asked us specifically if we had seen those men around town. We have a lot of freedom in this town, but Mom made it clear when we moved here that she trusted us with that freedom on the condition that we always told her the truth," Owen explained.

Vivian continued the explanation, "So, we had to tell her about the men in the boat, and she told us we would have to stay close to home until she had a chance to communicate with Dad."

"Finally, last night she was able to talk with him, and he told her it was okay for us to explore the town and hang out with you two. He didn't think we were in any danger, for now," Owen finished.

"For now?" Gabby didn't miss much.

* * *

For the rest of the morning, the friends sat at the picnic table and talked. Owen thought the new code would be just confusing enough that no one would be able guess the key, but simple enough to decode if you had the key. They talked about things they could do together. They had the whole summer ahead of them. Tomorrow was Sunday, so they planned to go swimming after church.

Gabby was happy that things seemed to be good between them. Owen was a sharp kid, and Gabby thought it might be a good idea to get his reaction to the playhouse event. "We had an interesting day yesterday," he began, and went on to explain about the cute cabin on the plant grounds and how it came to be there. "Jodie and I decided to go there to work on the code, and we found the place had been turned into a giant mess. Table and chairs overturned, drawers emptied on the floor, the bedding pulled off the bed with the mattress on the floor."

"The couch cushions thrown everywhere, and ashes dug out of the fireplace," Owen continued.

"Who told you about it?" Jodie looked at Owen with the same surprise as Gabby felt.

"Did you see Tim at the hardware store this morning?" Gabby was trying to make sense of Owen's words.

"Nobody had to tell us. That's what happens to our house every time we move into a new place," Vivian shoulders sagged. "We are really sorry to hear that our troubles are spilling over on you. Maybe we can't be friends after all." She looked sadly at the lovely flower bed along the edge of the park. The gentle sound of the flowing river added to the peacefulness of the place. The day was peaceful on the *outside*, anyway.

"Why would that change anything?" Jodie asked.

"It makes no difference to us." Gabby nodded at his twin in agreement. "The Eagle River Detectives thrive on trouble. You can count on them to save the day!"

"The Eagle River Detectives?" Owen asked. "Who are they?"

8

The Eagle River Detectives Explained

Gabby was surprised that their new friends had never heard of the Eagle River Detectives. "No one in town has said anything about how the detectives uncovered the true story about the Grant family and the manufacturing plant? You've never heard how Tim Grant became the hero of Eagle River?"

By now the friends had mounted their bikes and were pedaling lazily around the park as they talked. Occasionally, a bee buzzed their heads and just as quickly buzzed off to the nearby flowers that were everywhere along the park roadway.

"You mean your brother, Tim? You're saying he's some kind of town hero?" Vivian's blank look told the twins she knew nothing about any of it.

As they rode lazily, Gabby and Jodie took turns telling the amazing stories: how Carly refused to give up finding out why the townspeople didn't like them and were angry with their dad, and how Tim led the way to keeping a real disaster from hitting the town. They didn't neglect the part about their contributions to solving the cases, either.

"We worked as a team," Jodie said. You could hear the pride in her voice.

"We *work* as a team," Gabby corrected her. "And right now, our newest case involves the ransacking of our playhouse. Did your mom or dad ever say why they thought these men keep following you from town to town? They must be looking for something."

"Probably," Owen answered as he and Vivian exchanged glances. "We had better head home, Viv. Mom said not to be late." With that, the siblings peeled away from the twins and pedaled off toward town.

The day was getting hot, and the twins agreed it was time to head home for some ice-cold lemonade. As they rode up onto the lawn, Gabby turned to Jodie. "Was it my imagination, or did you feel like I did? The stories about the Eagle River Detectives didn't impress them—"

Jodie broke into her brother's thought. "It scared them."

* * *

Gabby and Jodie were out in the backyard, Ball at their feet. Each had a cold lemonade on the picnic table in front of them. This backyard table was where the Eagle River Detectives met most often to discuss their cases. The twins had considered calling a meeting but didn't feel like they had enough material to bring to the group.

"If we want to unravel the mystery behind these searches, we need a thread to pull. Somewhere to begin. What do we know so far?" Gabby asked thoughtfully.

"We saw those men with our own eyes, and it's likely they were checking up on Owen and Vivian. We know that the playhouse isn't the only place that has been searched, so somebody is looking for *something*. We can guess who the somebody is, but I don't have any idea what they are looking for, do you?" Jodie had summed up their frustration in a few sentences.

Ball looked at Gabby, hoping for some attention. Gabby rubbed the dog behind the ears. Ball gave him an adoring look, and without warning bolted for the front of the house. "Ball, you stupid dog." Gabby could just picture Tim trying to navigate his bike to safety with Ball winding into and out of his brother's path.

Hearing his name, Ball took off around the house and retrieved a ball from the backyard to take to Tim. Gabby and Jodie laughed out loud. It seemed the joke never got old. Hearing their laughter, Tim rounded the corner of the house and grabbed Gabby's untouched lemonade and gulped half the glass. "Thanks, bro." He winked at Gabby. "That was exactly what I needed after biking home in this heat after a long day's work." Tim plopped down next to Jodie. "What are you kids up to?" he asked.

Gabby began telling him about Owen and Vivian and the men who appeared to be after them. "And when we told them about the playhouse, Owen made the surprising admission that their house was ransacked every time they moved. I feel like we are in a game of hide and seek." Gabby needed a clue.

"Well," Tim said as he got up to go into the house to wash up for dinner. "If that's the case, all you have to do it figure out what is hiding."

* * *

Sunday morning found the whole family in church. After the service, Gabby and Jodie went to the fellowship hall in search of Gramps and Ernie. After going through the line for juice and a doughnut, the twins took their mini breakfast over to where the two men could be found almost every Sunday of the year.

"Hi, kids!" Ernie had a giant smile on his face. He loved having these kids in his life.

"Hi, Ernie. Hi, Gramps." Jodie smiled as she sat next to Gramps. Gabby grabbed a seat next to Ernie. "Did you hear about the excitement at the playhouse?" Gabby was curious to hear what theories the two men had about the event.

Gramps nodded and took a drink of his coffee. "Your mother said there didn't appear to be any real damage. That's a good thing."

"What do you think was going on, Ernie?" Gabby liked hearing from Ernie. He had been a detective for many years and looked below the surface when unusual things occurred.

"They were looking for something. That's where you have to start. It wasn't aimed at you kids; it was something they wanted to find. What's missing? And why did they think it could possibly be in the playhouse?" Ernie was often a step ahead of the kids. His observations gave them a way to move forward.

Jodie looked at Ernie and then at Grandpa. "So, the question is: why did someone search the cabin? That playhouse has been in this town longer than we have, so if there's something missing, it could have gone missing a long time ago."

"That's a great observation, little Missy." Ernie smiled approval on Jodie.

All around them people sat in friendly groups, enjoying the fellowship of the moment. Tim and Carly were talking with one of their friends from school.

Gramps chewed the last of his donut, and then clapped one hand on his knee. "Of course," he said, his eyes bright with delight as he drew a thought from his increasingly poor memory. "The map! They were looking for the treasure map!"

9

Something to Investigate

That evening, the Eagle River Detectives had a meeting. Gabby felt that he and Jodie needed input from the others and was pleased to find the others ready and waiting. Carly and Michael had come out with Tim and were already sitting at the picnic table out back. Ball was there, too, of course. He never missed a chance to be where the kids were and having them all in one spot was making his tail wag furiously as he ran circles around the table.

"Ball, cool it." Tim was tired of the dog's antics. Ball of course ran off to get Tim a ball.

The evening was warm, but there was a pleasant breeze. It felt good to be with the whole gang outside on a beautiful night. Gabby loved these sessions.

Carly usually ran the meetings and took notes. Tonight, however, she turned to Gabby. "Okay, little brother. Give us what you've got."

After Gramps blurted out the thing about the treasure map, he was unable to answer their questions to anyone's satisfaction. He insisted there was a map, though, and kept trying to get Ernie to explain it to everyone. "You know, Ernie," Gramps urged on his friend, "the treasure map. Everybody knew about it." Apparently, everybody but Ernie.

Ernie assured Gabby and Jodie he had no idea what Gramps was talking about, and Gramps clammed up after that. Gabby was eager to tell the group what they knew so far. Once they put their minds together, the Eagle River detectives were usually able to define their next move.

Gabby first told the others about Owen's revelation that, like the playhouse, his house had been ransacked every time they moved. This was news to the group.

"Okay, Gabby," Tim said, turning to his brother, "I'm going to have to agree with you that there is more to this than meets the eye."

Gabby and Jodie exchanged pleased looks. Jodie continued, "We all agreed that this was not an effort to vandalize, but a methodical search for something that someone hid. We think we know what it is…sort of."

"Sort of?" Michael asked.

"We asked Gramps and Ernie about the whole thing. Tim told us that if people are looking for something, it might be something that someone else has hidden. Gramps was finishing his donut and had one of those moments when you know he just remembered something." Gabby looked at the others to see how they were receiving the information.

"He said it had to be the treasure map," Jodie blurted out.

* * *

Once the other three members had expressed their surprise, Tim showed he had some misgivings about counting on information from Gramps. "You know Gramps' memory is getting worse every year," he cautioned. "Ernie has lived here all his life. Gramps said everyone knew about that treasure map, but Ernie didn't know anything about it."

Michael, as Carly's boyfriend, had been invited to be an official member of the club last year. He was pleased to be a part of the group but didn't often speak up in the meetings. So when he did speak, they listened. "I'm thinking about how your grandfather spent most of his adult life working at the furniture factory. Those were the folks he interacted with day in and day out. Maybe he meant everyone at the factory knew about the map."

"You're right, Michael," Carly agreed. "Gramps and Ernie barely knew each other until they became friends at Sumner place. Ernie could have easily been out of the loop."

"Out of the loop?" Jodie liked these sayings her older siblings used, but she sometimes needed them explained.

"It means that news travels from one person to another in a circular way and keeps going until most of the people are in on it. Ernie wouldn't have been around the people who were circulating the information, so he would be *out of the loop*." Tim pointed his finger toward the floor and drew an imaginary circle with his hand. "Get it?" Tim was good at breaking things down to where they made sense.

"Got it." Jodie gave Tim a thumbs up.

"I think it's time to start a few lists." Gabby knew Carly would have her pen and paper at the ready, so they could dig right in. "Any suggestions?"

Tim looked around the peaceful yard. Ball lay at his feet. It was still light out, but the birds were beginning their evening song. Gabby could tell that Tim wasn't happy to have another case so soon. Well, they didn't go looking for trouble, but as far as Gabby was concerned, when someone breaks into your property, you needed to find out what was going on.

Carly suggested they start with what they already knew and then write down a list of things they needed to find out. They knew that someone had searched the playhouse, and the search was very similar to Owen and Vivian's house being searched. They knew two strange men had been keeping an eye on the new kids and that it was because of their mom. They thought there was a treasure map because of Gramps. When they looked at that list, Gabby realized that they knew very little.

Jodie had the first question. "Is there anyone who used to work at the factory with Gramps that still remembers the treasure map?"

"Good one, Jodie," Carly praised her sister. "I've got another one. You said Owen and Vivian moved around a lot while their dad is stationed overseas. Why? And is there any special reason they go from place to place?"

"And is there a special reason they chose to move to Eagle River?" Tim was sharp.

"I'm going to add one," Gabby said. "Why did Owen and Vivian leave so quickly when they found out we were detectives?"

10

New Revelations

The next few days passed without incident. Summer was in full swing, and Gabby and Jodie spent most of their time at the park either swimming or fishing. They didn't see Owen or Vivian until Wednesday morning when Owen appeared, his fishing pole in hand.

"Vivian has swimming lessons this morning, but I thought maybe you two could give me some good fishing tips. I have to admit, I haven't had much luck on my own."

Gabby was surprised at how easily Owen jumped in and out of their friendship. Still, he was happy to see they were apparently on good terms again.

"Sure thing," he told Owen. "What have you got for bait?"

Jodie drifted over to a nearby picnic table and began to read the book she had just checked out of the library bookmobile.

If Vivian joined them after her lessons, Gabby was sure his twin would be happy to show Vivian how to check out

New Revelations

books. He was hoping this meant the friendship was back on for the summer. As they fished pleasantly, side by side, Gabby asked Owen one of the questions that had come up at the meeting.

"You said you have been moving quite a lot this past year. Is it any of my business to ask about that?" Gabby didn't want to upset his new friend again.

"Well, the first time, my grandma had surgery, and my mama needed to stay with her several months before she could get around on her own. Then, we went back to the base to live with my dad until he got sent overseas with the Army. After he left, we came here, since my mom remembered it as a nice place."

"What was her memory of Eagle River?" Jodie had caught on to the conversation and was standing by the river edge watching the boys fish.

"She has lots of memories," said Vivian as she pedaled over to the group, her swimming bag slung over her shoulder. "She went to high school here."

* * *

Gabby and Jodie had a lot to talk about after Vivian's bombshell disclosure. "Ms. Sampson lived in Eagle River when she was young, so she might know about the treasure map that Gramps was talking about. Maybe she came back to look for it." Jodie's head was spinning with ideas in light of this new information. "Or maybe she already has the map and that's why these guys are keeping tabs on her." Jodie's eyes lit up with this new thought.

Gabby's mind was working overtime as well. "I wonder if Mom remembers her. Owen and Vivian are about our age, so I guess their mom would be around our mom's age as well. If so, maybe Mom remembers the treasure map thing, too!" Things were getting exciting now that they had some new leads to follow.

The twins could barely wait for Mom to come home from work so they could ask her about Ms. Sampson. In the meantime, they biked over to Mason's Hardware store. Tim was unpacking a box of mosquito repellant to restock the shelf. It looked like he had another box to empty as well. Gabby could tell from the box labels that Tim would be filling the shelf with safety matches next. You could find about anything in that store. And that's why he wanted to talk with Tim.

"Hi, Tim," Jodie greeted her big brother. "We have a great new angle to take on the case, but you'll just have to wait until you get home to hear it." She loved to tease him.

Tim pulled his sister over where he could get good access and began to tickle her. "Tell me now, or you'll be tickled until it's time to go home."

Jodie freed herself easily and backed away from her tormenter, still laughing from being tickled.

Gabby shuffled his feet, waiting to get Tim's attention. Tim turned to his brother and put on his best work voice. "And how can I be of service to you, young man?"

Gabby went along with the silliness. "Good kind sir, could you help a young boy find a compass for his exploration needs?"

"My pleasure, lad," said Tim as he led the way to a row of shelves that had hunting supplies. Hanging on hooks on a large display board was a dazzling array of merchandise, including several compasses. "There you go, buddy. I have to get back to work." Tim could see Mr. Mason heading in their direction.

Gabby found the compass he wanted, and he and Jodie took it to the front to check out. Standing in line ahead of them was Tim's friend, Colin. "I see you're buying a compass," the boy said, examining Gabby's coming purchase. "I was really into that stuff a couple of years ago. My dad gave me a neat book on basic survival skills—things like how to start a fire without matches or how to find the north star at night so you know what direction you are going. It has a whole chapter on how to use a compass. You can borrow it if you want to." Colin was an only child, and his parents liked lavishing him with gifts. The nice thing about Colin was that he was very generous with his possessions.

"That would be great! Thanks, Colin." Jodie thought Colin, with his slightly shaggy brown hair and dark brown eyes, was quite charming and enjoyed it when he came to the house to hang out with Tim. "Maybe you could drop it off next time you come over."

"Sure thing." Colin liked all the Grant kids and enjoyed being a part of their busy household when he came over to hang out with Tim.

Ball saw the kids coming a block away and raced to greet them, weaving in and out of their bikes as they pedaled home. Carly and Michael were sitting on the porch swing talking as they swayed with the swing's movement. "Any news?" Michael asked.

Gabby could tell Michael was growing to like this detective business. "Yes, but we're not going to say what it is until Mom comes home from work. I think you will find our conversation with Mom very interesting."

11

An Enlightening Mealtime

Shortly after the twins got home, Colin swung by on his moped with the book he had promised. "You can keep it if you like," he told them. "Now that I know what is in it, I can just look the information up on the internet if I need my memory refreshed."

Colin took a seat on a chair on the porch and settled in for a talk with Michael and Carly until Tim came home from work. He needed Tim's signature in order to sign up for a softball tournament in which they had agreed to play.

After thanking Colin, Gabby and Jodie went upstairs to read about compasses and begin to learn how to use one. Detectives needed special skills that other people might not need was Jodie's way of putting it. In other words, "Be prepared." The twins had adopted it as their motto. Jodie even drew the words in big letters on a sheet of paper and had hung it on the wall by her desk. Gabby heard Carly say she thought it was a little melodramatic. He had to look that word up. There were several definitions: theatrical, over dramatic, hammy, and exaggerated were some he remembered. But since there was one definition that was *cloak-and-dagger,* Gabby decided that described their detective business just fine, so they let it stand.

"There are a lot of things in this book that we need to master if we want to be able to help ourselves in any situation." Jodie was very excited by Colin's gift. They began on the page about compasses. Time passed quickly, and before long, the smell of meatloaf and fresh bread wafted up the stairs, into the bedroom, into their noses, and into their brains. "That smells awesome," said Gabby. "Let's go get some dinner!"

As they entered the inviting room, they were surprised to see Gramps and Ernie already seated at the large kitchen table. Papa John was helping Carly and Michael prepare the food for the table.

"Carly said she was making Grandma's famous fresh bread and needed me to be the first to try it to see if she did it right. I'll never turn down a chance to taste a recipe from your Gram. I sure miss her cooking. Ernie, of course offered to be a taster, too, so here we are!" Gramps explained their presence.

"Coming," Mom called out as she came in the front door. Of them all, Mom was most often late to the table these days. She worked long hours at the factory but made sure to be home for the evening meal, even if she was not always on time.

"Me, too!" Tim walked into the kitchen behind his mother and took a seat by Gabby. "Hi, Gramps. Hi, Ernie. To what do we owe this honor?"

Gramps explained again about the bread tasting he and Ernie were there to do. When they first moved to Eagle River, the kids had lived with Gramps while their mom was working outside of the country, and their meals always began with their grandfather offering a prayer of thanksgiving for the food. And that was how this meal began tonight as well. "Amen," everyone joined in as he finished.

Once the eating began, the family spent most of their time enjoying the food. Gabby was sure that Carly would have gotten a big thumbs up on the freshly baked bread even without Gramps' raving review. Ernie just sat there with a big smile on his face as he feasted on a thick slice of the loaf slathered with strawberry jam.

As they finished the meal with apple cake for dessert, the conversation began to flow. Gabby started things off by talking about their new friends, Owen and Vivian. "They told us they had moved around a lot in the past few months. We asked what brought them to Eagle River." Gabby took a leisurely forkful of cake.

Tim looked at his brother impatiently. "Okay, I'll bite. What brought them to Eagle River?"

"Their mom went to high school here," Jodie said.

* * *

"When we told Owen and Vivian about the break-in at the playhouse, they said they could picture exactly how it looked, because the last three places they lived had been searched, just like our playhouse had. Jodie and I figure that if their mom used to live in Eagle River that might explain why the playhouse got searched. So, how about it, Mom.

Did you know her when she lived here? If so, would there have been a time that she visited the playhouse?"

"I don't know the answer to your question." Mom's brows were drawn together as she tried to picture a friend or acquaintance that fit the twins' description. "Someone who would have been at the playhouse, you think."

"Vivian said her mom's name was Lila." Jodie offered.

"Lila Decker! I remember her now. She was a grade behind me. She and I were cheerleaders together one year." Mom smiled as though the memories she was revisiting were pleasant ones. "And, at the end of the season I invited the whole cheer squad over to the playhouse for an overnight. We had so much fun."

"I knew it," Gabby said triumphantly. "There is a connection."

Tim was not willing to jump to conclusions so easily. "How in the world would the people who searched the playhouse know about a cheerleader party and who was in attendance? That is ancient history." Seeing the look on his mother's face after that comment, he rushed to cover his mistake. "No offense, Mom."

"Ancient history, indeed," Mom scolded her eldest son, while everyone else had a good laugh at Tim's expense. "Except for the *ancient history* part, though, I tend to agree with Tim," she added.

"We have another question, Mom." Carly thought this might be a good time to ask. "Do you remember any gossip about a treasure map back in those years?"

Gramps turned toward his daughter as though wanting confirmation to his earlier claim.

Papa John and Mom exchanged a startled glance. "How did you kids stumble onto that rumor. That was so long ago." Mom's answer seemed evasive to Gabby. The table got silent.

"You mean that it was so long ago that that story is pretty much *ancient history?*" Tim teased. Everyone laughed at that, and the joke served to break the tension.

"Let's just say I'd like you kids to forget whatever it is you heard about the map, and just leave it alone." The kids could tell Mom was serious. Gabby, however, took note that Mom had said *she would like it* if they did nothing about it, but she didn't exactly forbid them to continue the investigation. Leaving things unsolved was not in the Eagle River Detectives' DNA.

12

A Day in the Woods

After the meal was over, the kids helped clear the table. Tim and Gabby put the dishes in the dishwasher, Michael and Carly put away the food, and Jodie swept the floor. Mom said the dishes weren't done until the floor was swept, which made no sense, but the kids knew what she meant: if you were in charge of clean-up, it included a clean floor.

The twins found Mom relaxing on the recliner in the living room, having a rousing visit with Gramps and Ernie who sat on the couch. Those two always had stories of funny things that happened at the assisted living where they each had a room. Gramps explained that Donna, the lady in the room next to Ernie, was very hard of hearing. Ernie overheard one of the aides complement the woman: "You look pretty in pink," the young girl had said. Ernie said Donna's head swiveled toward the aide and asked, "You think I stink?" The flustered aide made sure to speak a lot

A Day in the Woods

louder after that so that Donna would hear her right the first time.

"Good one, Ernie," Gabby said, laughing with the others.

After things settled down a bit, Gabby had a question for his mother. "Is it okay if Jodie and I bike over to the factory tomorrow with Owen and Vivian and explore the woods behind the property? We're working on our outdoor skills. In particular, we want to try out the new compass I bought with my birthday money. Colin gave us a book about how to use it, and we'd like to try it out."

"That would be fine, and thanks for clearing it with me ahead of time. Since the incident at the playhouse, we have upped our surveillance, and I don't want anyone to be alarmed that someone is in the woods." Mom never just let things slide. She was determined not to let something like that break-in happen on the factory property a second time.

They would meet Owen and Vivian at the park and ride out to the factory together.

* * *

The morning was sunny with a slight breeze that staved off the heat. The weather forecast predicted a few clouds toward evening with isolated showers possible, but for now, the day was perfect. After collecting Owen and Vivian from the park, they headed out of town, riding past farm fields. The vast rows of corn were forming nicely as far as the eye could see. Gramps told Gabby that the old saying that the corn needed to be "knee-high by the Fourth of July." This was closer to the fourth of June. The kids parked their bikes in the ditch by one of the fields next to the road and climbed over the wooden fence. As they stood in one of the rows next to the growing corn, they found the cornstalks had *already* grown higher than their knees. Gabby would be sure to report that to Gramps and Ernie on his next visit. In Nebraska, corn was a huge crop, and cornfields were a familiar sight to anyone who traveled the rural roads of the state. The twins liked knowing that Nebraska's farmers helped feed the world.

Back on their bikes they could see the factory in the distance. The woods at the far end of the buildings covered a large area. A creek ran through the terrain, making it unsuitable for farming, but the ready water from the creek accounted for the growth of the trees. Grampa Grant had left the area undisturbed as a natural habitat for the animals and birds that made their homes there. Beaver, muskrat, deer, pheasant, and even turkeys lived and thrived in the lush haven. Gabby was surprised he and Jodie hadn't thought to explore the place until now.

They rolled through the factory gates, waving to the security guard in the little guardhouse that regulated traffic in and out of the property. Mom must have informed the man they were coming, because he just smiled and waved them through. They rode on past the playhouse, past the loading docks, and all the way to where the road became rough and bumpy. From there on, the road was primitive. Gabby knew it was basically a cleared path that would allow a vehicle to exit to the road from the back of the factory when necessary.

A Day in the Woods

They parked their bikes at the edge of the woods and followed a path that eventually led to the creek. Gabby unpacked the compass from his backpack. He and Jodie had been reading about compasses in the book from Colin, and one of the things it emphasized was keeping the compass away from other magnetic instruments. That meant keeping it away from cell phones, computers, and other electrical devises that could create magnetic fields. Gabby didn't have a cell phone, but there were electrical devises on the gates at the factory that he did not want to risk exposing it to. Also, dropping the compass could cause it to malfunction. That's why he had it wrapped carefully in his backpack.

"We should figure out which direction is north from this spot. That way we can draw up a map of the woods as we explore it," Gabby suggested. The four children gathered around the compass. "The needle is painted red at the tip, and points North because of the magnetism of the north pole. If we line up the wheel, where it says north with the tip, we will be able to see the other directions as well. South is opposite north, and east and west are on either side: East to the right of North and west to the left." Jodie had told Gabby many times that he would make a good teacher and reminded him repeatedly that in school the teachers got to do most of the talking.

Jodie took out a tablet, prepared to draw the map. "The book said that a map is always drawn with the top of the map facing north." Jodie sat down on a fallen log and turned the paper to match the direction of the red dial on the compass. She wrote North at the top of the page. The creek was running next to the tablet in the same direction of the compass.

"In that case," Owen said, "right in this spot the creek is running north and south." Jodie drew the creek extending from the top of the page to the bottom. "When we came into the woods, we walked in a straight line to get to the creek, so the path from the factory runs east and west. The factory is east of where we are standing." Jodie drew a path coming in from the right side of the page to the creek.

"As long as we can find our way back to the creek, we can figure out how to get back to the factory because the compass will tell us which way is north," Vivian said in delight. "We are real woodsmen now," she added proudly.

Jodie continued to mark things on her map as they explored the woods. There was an old woodshed that looked like it was ready to fall over. When Owen managed to get the door about half-way open, they could see that there was a fair amount of wood still in the ramshackle building. "We have to remember that when we need wood for the fireplace that's in the playhouse," Gabby noted.

As they drew further into the woods, they began to hear rustling in the underbrush. They spotted the occasional squirrel here and there, and bees and dragonflies buzzed overhead. The chirping birds sang sweetly. The shade was a welcome addition as the day grew warmer. All in all, the forest was a pleasant place to be on a lovely summer day. *Why didn't I think of exploring this place sooner?* Gabby chided himself again.

Vivian was the first to spot the treehouse. "How do we get up there?" she asked. It was a nice structure, but not situated where you could climb the tree to reach it. Jodie circled the tree and found a rope ladder attached to a platform that held the cute house. Gabby tried it out. The rope seemed safe. He climbed up first with Owen right behind him. Jodie studied the tree's position in relation to the woodshed and the creek and marked it carefully on the map. She figured they would want to be able to find the right tree the next time they came looking for the treehouse.

"What's it like?" Vivian was looking up at the boys with her hand shading her eyes from the sun.

"Come on up and check it out for yourself," Owen invited. Vivian and Jodie made their way up the ladder and on to the landing. As they peeked in the doorway, they saw the boys deep in discussion about something they had found tacked to the treehouse wall. It was a map.

13

The Map

"Is it the treasure map?" Jodie looked like she could hardly breathe; she was so excited. She and Vivian stormed the door and rushed to where the boys were standing. The map was about the size of the poster board the twins had used for a science project on tree leaves. Not huge, but bigger than the paper in the tablet on which Jodie was drawing her map. It did not tell you much.

"What is all that stuff?" Vivian couldn't make sense of any of it.

Owen and Gabby had had more time to examine the drawings. "We think it's definitely in code but using pictures rather than letters of the alphabet," Gabby told the girls.

"The problem is we're not sure we can even guess what the pictures are, not to mention what they represent in code," Owen added. "Here, take my place and see if you can make anything of it."

The Map

The two girls moved in to study the map close up. The boys hovered behind them, still trying to interpret the meaning behind the drawings.

"The first building looks a bit like the loading docks at the back of the factory," Jodie mused. That was where the trucks backed up to the warehouse so that the furniture could be transferred on to the trucks and shipped to their destinations. Several stick figures were playing catch at the side of the building where Mom had told them used to be a softball field.

"The next building looks like a house, but the rest of the shapes are too scribbly to look like much of anything." Vivian still couldn't make sense of it and was ready to move on. "Are we going to explore the rest of the woods or not?"

The boys, too, had lost interest. "It's definitely not a treasure map," Gabby announced. "No X marks the spot on that crazy thing. Let's see if we can find how far it is to the edge of the woods."

The kids scrambled nimbly down the ladder, being careful not to hurt their hands on the rough roping. Owen suggested they follow the creek, which they did. It stayed cool under the shade of the trees. Wildflowers peeked out from the undergrowth of grasses and old leaves. The air smelled moist from the water in the nearby creek. It was a pleasant hike and, eventually, they reached the edge of the woods. This was where the old road led out to the highway. Rather than retrace their steps, they followed the road back to the plant and collected their bikes for the ride home. It was nearly supper time, and Owen said that exploring made him hungry.

"Everything makes you hungry," teased Jodie.

As they pedaled home, they were tired but content. It had been a good day. Gabby felt like there was something he should have noticed back there. "Maybe we should have tried to copy the map to show Carly and Tim," he said.

"Better yet, let's come back here soon with the whole gang and see what they make of things," Jodie suggested. "Tim will have his phone along, and he can easily take a picture of the map."

Gabby smiled at his twin. She always had good ideas.

14

Tim and Gabby Make a Good Team

At breakfast the next morning, Carly and Jodie began a talk about shoes. "What do you look for in good shoes for summer?" Jodie asked her big sister, looking over Carly's shoulder as she scrolled through shoe styles on one of her favorite footwear sites.

"Well, it depends on if you mean everyday flipflops or dressy sandals," Carly answered vaguely.

Gabby ate his cereal, bored with the breakfast table conversation. Jodie was excited that Carly was going to take her on a girl's day shopping trip, and that meant Gabby had to find something to do on his own. He had gotten used to Jodie planning their schedule for the day and was trying to figure out what he would do until the girls returned from their shopping excursion. "I hope you have a wonderful time, girls," Gabby said in a snarky tone of voice, obviously irritated by their happy chatter.

Tim strolled into the kitchen just then, grabbed a bowl, and plopped down next to his little brother. "You sound grumpy this morning." Tim jabbed Gabby with his elbow.

"He's just being annoying because we're going shopping, and he doesn't want to go along. But he doesn't know what to do with himself without Jodie there to fill in his activity calendar." Carly liked to tease, too.

"Well, bro, you are in luck," Tim smiled at his scowling brother. "I don't work today, and I was hoping I could find a free sibling to hang out with. What do you say? Can I be your Jodie substitute for the day?"

Gabby looked at his brother with wide eyes and a big grin. "Just you and me?" The day had taken a huge turn for the better. "That would be awesome."

The girls watched in amusement as Gabby's face went from glum to sunny in about two seconds. Gabby looked at Tim to be sure he had heard him right.

"Yep. Just you and me," Tim smiled at a now happy Gabby. As Tim finished his cereal, the girls left the room to do whatever girls do to go shopping. Gabby got up, rinsed his empty bowl, and put it in the dishwasher. "I was hoping you would have time to come out to the factory with me. I want to show you the woods we were exploring and get your opinion on something we found out there. If you bring your phone, we can take a picture of it."

"Now you have me intrigued. I'll run upstairs and grab my phone and meet you out front," Tim said taking the stairs three at a time.

Gabby was an expert at springing surprises, and he knew Tim wouldn't back out if he made the trip seem mysterious. Tim was Gabby's hero. Sometimes Gabby struggled with his own identity. He felt he could never live up to Tim's example. He pictured himself as the little, talkative brother who needed his twin around to feel complete. *What a loser.*

Tim and Gabby set out for the factory grounds at a leisurely pace. Gabby could tell that Tim was enjoying the bike ride as much as he was. The morning air was still crisp, and Gabby was glad he had grabbed a lightweight jacket at the last moment. The boys were silent as they sped through the mostly deserted streets. As they reached the outskirts of town, Tim broke the silence with a low whistle. "Just look at that corn," he said in amazement. "It's almost up to my knees."

Gabby was surprised to see that the cornstalks looked even taller than when he last passed the field. A lot could happen before the fall harvest, but if it kept growing at this rate this farmer could look forward to a bumper crop.

"Last time we made sure to tell Mom we were going to be in the woods, and she thanked us for letting her know," Gabby informed his brother as they sailed through the front gate.

"Sure thing," said Tim. The boys parked their bikes near the entrance to the main building and walked up the stairs to Mom's office.

"Well, this is a nice surprise." Mom smiled as the boys came through the door. "What are you two doing here? Already bored with summer?"

"Not in the least," said Tim as he wandered over to the big window that looked out over the factory floor below.

Tim loved the factory and couldn't wait until he was old enough to work in the family business.

"We just wanted to let you know we are going to explore the woods again today," Gabby told his mother. "Tim couldn't come last time, and Carly and Jodie went shopping. It's neat back there."

"I don't know much about the woods, but I know your father used to love to explore out there," Mom said with a faraway look as though remembering a different time.

"Well, Gabby is going to give me the big tour, so we should let you get back to work." Tim headed for the stairs and Gabby followed eagerly. He was pleased to know that Dad had liked the woods, too. Maybe Gabby wasn't a total loser.

Gabby took the lead and Tim seemed content to follow. Having his big brother tagging along behind *him* for a change made Gabby smile. Tim parked his bike next to Gabby's near the edge of the trees.

"Colin and I ventured near here a couple of times when the plant was all locked up and we were doing a lot of exploring, but at that time the buildings held our full attention," Tim told Gabby as he looked around at the layout. "I knew there was a road back here, but I don't think I knew there was a creek."

"I'll show you the way to the creek, which runs north and south, by the way." Gabby entered the woods, happy to be in the lead once again. "We used my new compass to figure that out. The compass showed that the factory is due east of the creek." Gabby was babbling happily.

The forest was as mysterious and welcoming as last time. Tim seemed to catch the magic of the place, too. "I love the way the sun makes its way between the tree branches, leaving the forest floor looking like it's decorated in random patterns of light."

Gabby looked at his brother in surprise. "That sounds like something someone would write in a poem. My brother, the poet." Gabby swept his arm gracefully as though giving Tim an introduction to an audience.

Tim looked around at the trees and wildflowers. The only spectators were the birds singing happy songs from high in the trees. "I think a beautiful place like this can bring out the poet in all of us," he said, not in the least embarrassed by Gabby's teasing. "I can see why you and Dad are drawn to this place. It's beautiful. Peaceful, too."

The two boys walked among the trees. Sometimes Tim led and sometimes Gabby. As they neared the treehouse Gabby forged ahead. He wanted to see if Tim would spot the treehouse on his own. As he suspected, Tim walked right under the structure without noticing it.

Gabby held out his hand, palm to the front showing he wanted Tim to stop. "We almost missed the surprise," he informed his big brother. "Look up."

"Wow, a treehouse! How do we get up there?"

Gabby happily showed his brother the rope ladder hidden from view on the other side of the big tree trunk. He let Tim go up first, scrambling nimbly behind him. It was close, but Tim could still stand upright in the structure if he stayed toward the middle where the peaked roof rose the highest. Mom said Tim was not done growing yet, and she wouldn't be surprised if he passed the six-foot mark on the "track your growth" chart on the wall of their bedroom.

Tim looked out the windows to check the view. The trees were in full leaf, and you could barely see cornfields peeking in at the far end of the woods. Spotting the poster on the wall, he went over to examine it.

"That's what I wanted to show you. What do you make of it?" Gabby asked his brother.

"I don't know. It's primitive. The loading docks. The kids playing ball. Some kind of house. I can't even make out what the other scribbles could be." Tim saw about the same thing all the other kids had seen.

Crack! "What was that?" Gabby didn't think a small animal could make a sound that decisive.

Tim was back at the window looking for movement in the woods. The silence was now as loud as the noise had been. "If I had to guess, it sounded like someone stepping on a dry piece of wood and snapping it in half. If that's what it was, then we have company," Tim whispered. By mutual consent the boys stayed very still for several minutes, listening for other sounds. Just as they were about to give up, they heard a truck motor start about where the dirt road re-entered the highway. "I think they're gone now," Tim said.

"And if they left without making themselves known, they probably didn't belong back here," said Gabby. "Instead of taking a picture, why don't we take the map with us. Maybe it will make more sense when we have more clues."

Tim went over and removed the tacks holding the map in place as Gabby lifted it from the wall. As he turned, Tim made a low whistle. Gabby looked at him with a question in his eyes.

"The treasure map is on the back, bro."

15

The Real Map

The two boys rushed the poster board to the flat surface of the table in the center of the treehouse. Now that they had it in good light, Gabby was sure it was the real deal. "I wonder if there is a real treasure chest, too." Gabby's eyes were glued to the new find, his face alight with excitement.

Tim was excited, too, but he warned Gabby that finding the map was just the first step in what might turn out to be a hard road to finding the treasure. Tim was probably thinking about Gramps' revelation that lots of people before them had already been on the hunt.

Gabby had to agree. First of all, the images on the map seemed random. It looked like a board game, like Candy Land maybe, with paths leading to different areas, but this game didn't come with directions. Each step on the treasure hunt was hidden in several layers of clues. At first glance, it made no sense. This was going to take the whole group's effort, and even then, they might not ever figure it out.

The Real Map

"I say we take it home, get the Eagle River Detectives together, and talk through each of the images as the first step in figuring this thing out." Tim knew this would be no easy task. "You start down first, and I can hand the map down to you as you get close to the ground."

"Good plan." Gabby carefully rolled up the map. It would be easier to transport it that way. He knelt next to the rope ladder to gauge the distance. They could just about do it. If Tim reached out his arm to full length and extended the map toward Gabby, Gabby's outstretched arm should be able to grab the end nicely. Gabby scrambled down the ladder. It seemed shakier this time, but he was better at using it after having been up and down several times now. Standing on the last rung, he reached up for the treasure map. He could feel it touch his fingertips. "Just a little more and I've got it."

Tim stretched out over the edge holding on to the ladder to steady himself and was able to lower the precious find into Gabby's firm grasp. "Well done, brother,' Gabby looked up at Tim, waving the prize. Tim put his foot firmly on the first rung of the rope and then the second, at the third rung the rope snapped and Tim came flying down to the ground with a thud.

"Tim?" said a shaken Gabby. Tim didn't move.

* * *

Gabby didn't want to have to go through a time like that again for the rest of his life. Grabbing Tim's phone, he had called Mom, and she had called 911. Mom and one of the security guards had found their way to the woods where an anxious Gabby waited at the edge and then led the way to Tim, who still wasn't moving. By the time the ambulance arrived—*it took f-o-r-e-v-e-r*—Tim had begun to moan and had opened his eyes a little. The three of them were the first thing Tim saw as he began to return to consciousness. "What happened?" the woozy boy asked.

Gabby dropped down to sit on the ground next to his brother, finally able to let go of some of the tension in his body at the relief of hearing Tim's voice. "It'll be okay. Mom's here and help is on the way."

By the time the paramedics had Tim on a stretcher and were carrying him to the ambulance for a trip to the hospital, Tim had come fully awake. He could move both of his arms and legs, though he still seemed a bit out of it. That was the point at which Gabby had relaxed. God had been there with them the whole time, answering his frantic prayers and taking care of Tim. Gabby was trusting that God would continue to be with them. He had said a heartfelt prayer of thanks to a kind and gracious God then and continued to thank Him later as he sat on his bed, watching his brother sleeping peacefully on the bed next to his. Gabby felt like it had been his fault Tim had gotten hurt. He should have let Tim go first. The rope would have held his weight better if Gabby hadn't already put stress on it by going down first.

The doctor had checked Tim thoroughly and found that, while he had a slight concussion from hitting his head as he landed, he seemed otherwise okay—a few bangs and bruises, but nothing that wouldn't fully heal. They were to watch him for a couple of days. Hitting one's head was nothing to mess around with, but if Tim seemed to steadily improve and had no bouts of confusion, the doctor felt he should be fine.

Gabby looked with surprise at the rolled map in his hand. He had been carrying it around with him this whole time and hadn't given it a thought. Thoughts of a grand treasure paled next to the treasure sleeping peacefully at his side. God has a way of putting things in perspective. Tim was the real treasure.

* * *

Tim woke up from his nap feeling a lot better. He said his head still hurt a bit, but nothing that he couldn't live with. Gabby asked if he felt up to having an Eagle River Detective meeting after the evening meal. The rest of the kids said they could make it if Tim felt well enough. Tim said he was fine with that, so Gabby informed the others they were good to go.

When Gabby and Mom had been at the hospital waiting for Tim to come back from the x-ray department—the doctor was making sure he had no broken bones from the fall—Mom scolded him. "I thought I had made it clear that I did not want you kids to have anything to with that treasure map business."

"But, Mom," Gabby started to explain.

"Don't *but* me," Mom cut him off.

"Mom, I just want to clear up a couple of things before you jump to conclusions," Gabby pleaded.

One thing Gabby appreciated about his mother was that she usually tried to be fair. "Okay, but this better be good," she relented.

"First of all, we didn't go into the woods looking for the treasure map. I wanted to show Tim the treehouse we discovered. It's true that there was a map on the wall of the treehouse, but it wasn't that kind of a map. It was a couple of sloppy drawings. Jodie and I had already seen it with Owen and Vivian the other day when we went exploring. It seemed pointless, but after Tim saw it, we decided to take it along with us in case it really was a clue.

"Then we heard a sound like someone had snapped a branch by stepping on it. We listened for a while and didn't hear anything more except for a truck starting up by the road in back. We didn't think any more about it. If anyone had been in the woods, they were gone by then. I held the poster board while Tim pulled out the tacks, and when I turned to take the map down, Tim saw the back…and there was the real map. When I went down the rope ladder it was a little wobbly, but when Tim got halfway down, the rope broke, throwing him to the ground."

"Oh, no," Mom said. "Another accident connected to that crazy map."

"I don't know anything about other accidents," Gabby said, as he looked intently at his mother. But this was no accident. I checked the rope. It was cut."

16

What's Next?

Tim continued to feel okay the rest of the day, so after supper, the group met at the picnic table in the backyard. Carly's boyfriend, Michael, was there along with all of Gabby's siblings. Gabby and Tim had filled them in over supper. Mom had been insistent that they stay away from anything that involved the treasure map. Up until then, she had not given them any reason to quit, but that evening she told them about the trouble the map had caused so many years ago.

"I don't remember all the details, but Dad, that's Gramps to you, would come home from the plant almost daily with stories about people having accidents because of that stupid map. One time, one of the ladies fell down the office stairs and broke her leg trying to follow a clue. Another time I remember a young man who worked in the assembly line had a bad bicycle accident on one of the country roads near the golf course looking for some obscure shed where he thought the treasure might be hidden.

Another time Gramps himself was knocked out when someone hit him over the head when he went into a small room off the loading dock. It got so bad your grandfather Grant had to make a company rule against treasure hunting on factory property." Gabby could tell Mom was still upset by the memories. "You kids have to stop, right now," she ordered. "It's not safe."

Gabby exchanged a knowing look with Tim. "Tim and I talked through everything that happened, and we think it might be more dangerous to let it go, than to solve the mystery."

Mom stood up, hand on hips. She was having none of it. "That's ridiculous."

"Here's our thinking," Tim explained. "When Gabby and I went up into the treehouse, we had no intention of finding anything. Gabby just wanted to show me the treehouse. But whoever was in the woods that day probably knew that we are the kids who uncovered a couple of mysteries in this town already, so they just assumed we were looking for the treasure and tried to sabotage us. We think they might have been behind all those "accidents" you told us about as well. That means they are serious about finding the treasure and will stop at nothing to get it."

"Which is exactly why I want you to stop." Mom put her hands to her head as though to say, *"What part of this don't you get?"*

"What Tim is trying to say is that whoever is behind this still thinks we are on the trail of the treasure, and we won't be safe from their attacks no matter whether we finish this or leave it alone. Plus, we were caught by surprise this time, but now we know to be careful." Gabby could see that his mother had not considered this angle.

Papa John looked at his wife with his head turned to the side, as though thinking, and his hands flat together in front of his mouth. "They have a point you know."

"I guess there is no proof that one course of action is any safer than another," Mom reluctantly conceded.

"We'll be careful," Carly promised. "Michael and I will keep an eye out for anything that seems dangerous and will call a halt if things turn ugly."

Jodie took Gabby's hand and gave it a squeeze as if to say, "I'm ready. Let's do this!"

* * *

Tim was looking tired so they knew this meeting would be a short one, but everyone was anxious to look at the treasure map. Gabby carefully unrolled the poster board to display the back side where he and Tim had found the map.

Michael was already working at the factory and pointed out that all the references looked to be in the factory building itself. That didn't mean they could make sense of it though. "This isn't any more helpful than the other side was," a disappointed Jodie groaned as she stomped her foot in frustration.

"Rather than trying to figure this out tonight, let's sleep on it," Carly suggested, nodding toward Tim whose eyes were only half open. They could all see he needed to rest. "We visit Gramps and Ernie tomorrow. Maybe seeing the map will trigger a memory in Gramps' mind."

Gabby brought up the accidents Mom had let slip at the supper table. "Maybe Gramps can fill us in on what that was about. Tim's fall was no accident, that's for sure."

Everyone looked at Gabby in surprise. That's when he remembered to tell them about the noise he and Tim had heard in the woods and about the rope being cut.

17

Gramps, Dear Gramps

Gabby woke up the next morning with his confidence shaken. He had been taking the lead in this investigation but now wondered if he was leading the group into unnecessary danger. *What would be the worst thing that could happen if they just let the whole thing go?* Well, Owen and Vivian would still be under the watch of whoever those men were. That's what started everything in the first place. Plus, if they backed off now, they would always wonder who had done the damage to the playhouse. And, like he and Tim had reasoned with Mom, how did they know that by getting the Eagle River Detectives to end the search that the guys who had tried to hurt them by cutting the rope ladder would leave them alone? Besides, Tim and Carly would never back down, he decided, and neither would he. He might not be much, but he was a Grant. As Dad used to say, "Buck up or get out of the truck."

Tim had gotten permission to work a half day. Both Mom and Mr. Mason, Tim's boss, agreed that he should take it easy for a few more days. That meant he was already home at lunchtime, and they could go to the assisted living to see Gramps and Ernie earlier than usual. The map was spread out in the center of the kitchen table, and as they began to be more familiar with it, they started to form some of the questions they hoped Gramps could answer. Carly had her notepad out and pen poised as they compiled a list. If people had a favorite word, like they had a favorite color, Carly's word would be "list."

Jodie offered up the first suggestion. "Let's ask Gramps if there are any stairs at the plant other than the obvious ones leading up to the office." A vision of Carly and Tim being trapped in that office flew through Gabby's mind. That had happened in their first case, when they had helped clear their dad's name. The memory sent a sliver of fear down Gabby's spine.

"Good one." Carly wrote the question down. "I want to ask why Mom thinks that the guy that got hurt in the bicycle accident back then was connected to the treasure map." She wrote that down as well.

"Are there small rooms we don't know about that could hide the treasure?" Tim added his thought. "And Mom said Gramps got knocked out. Where did that happen?" As Gabby added this question, he felt another shiver. This case was turning out to have a dangerous side. *Dear God, help us to know if this is something we should pursue or not.* The prayer slipped out easily. Gabby counted on God being ready to hear his prayers wherever and whenever he prayed. Most of his courage came from knowing that he was under God's loving eye. He had just memorized a new Bible passage from the book of Joshua in Sunday School and he had decided it was one of his favorites. It said, "Have I not commanded you, be strong and courageous. Do not be discouraged, do not be afraid, for the Lord your God is with you wherever you may go" (Joshua 1:9).

Gabby thought of it as God's version of his dad's, "Buck up or get out of the truck," slogan, only with the added promise that God would protect them, which was why they could be brave.

Michael was coming, too. Gabby hoped Ernie would be at Gramps' side when they got there so that the whole gang was together. Moving to the assisted living had been a good move for Gramps. Because they did things much the same way every day, Gramps was able to keep up with the daily routine, and having Ernie around pleased both men. Gabby loved these visits.

As usual, Gramps and Ernie were outside in the park-like area behind the building. They were sitting near the gazebo where summer flowers waved gently in the breeze. The men were in deep conversation and didn't see the small group approaching them.

"Boo," said Gabby, playfully. Both the men's bodies tensed, and they looked at Gabby, eyes wide. *Was that fear he saw in their eyes?* Gabby wondered.

"Don't sneak up on us like that," Gramps scolded the kids mildly. "We've had enough scary events to last us for a while."

Carly looked at Gramps and then at Ernie. "What *scary events* are we talking about here? I didn't think assisted living places had *scary events*." Gabby could tell Carly was alarmed.

Gramps and Ernie exchanged a look that told Gabby that the two men had already decided not to share that information during this visit. "Busted, you two." Tim had noticed the glance as well. "Enlighten us."

Annoyed at himself, Gramps looked at Ernie apologetically. "Oh, that," he said, stalling.

"It's okay, Bill," Ernie told his friend. "These Eagle River Detectives are sharp. They would have gotten the info out of us one way or another." Looking at the kids' concerned faces, Ernie knew they would worry even more if they didn't give them the story. "Yesterday evening, when your grandpa went back to his room after supper, he found two men digging through his belongings. When he yelled at them to get out of his room, they ran through the doorway, almost knocking him off his feet.

"When he told me about it, we went together to tell the supervisor, and she wouldn't believe us. She said your Gramps was often confused, and this had to be another of those times. She assured us that the building was always locked, and visitors had to be buzzed through the door by someone unlocking the door from inside. She was the one to let the visitors in this evening, and she had not let anyone in that she did not recognize."

"Does Mom know about this?" Jodie was obviously shaken by the story, and Gabby knew Mom would be upset that she had not been informed.

Now he felt really bad. Had Gramps been drawn into danger because of him? Gabby was the one who had wanted a new case and had gotten them involved in this whole treasure hunt idea.

"We didn't tell her, and the supervisor was so sure it couldn't have happened that she didn't call your mother either," Ernie explained.

Carly looked at both sharply. "You said scary *things*, plural. More than one, right? Come on, Gramps, what else are you not telling us?" Gabby could tell Carly was really upset.

"You kids don't miss much, do you? I guess I haven't mentioned seeing those same men lurking by the gazebo when I came out to meet with Ernie to wait for your visit," Gramps confessed. "I am not afraid of them. I don't think they are here to hurt me, but I hate the feeling of someone watching me or looking through my things."

"That makes our visit today take on new importance," Michael told the two men. "We want to ask you about the people injured while the treasure hunting craze was going on at the factory so many years ago. These men may not be out to harm you, but people have been hurt in the past and the present."

Gabby told the men about finding the map, and Tim falling from the cut ladder. Gramps and Ernie sat enthralled. Ernie slapped his knee in delight when they told of finding the real map on the back of the sloppy one and gasped at the tale of Tim's fall. When Gabby finished, the group fell silent. Gramps tapped his fingers on the arm of his chair, deep in thought. Gabby realized that he was holding his breath, hoping that Gramps remembered something.

"Well," he began slowly, "the lady who broke her leg coming down the stairs from the office worked in the packaging area, so it was not common for her to be in the office. I guess she could have been hunting the treasure. I remember your grandfather Grant complaining about those crazy visits. People started to come in randomly and stand by the window that looked out over the factory floor. That stopped after he forbad the hunt." Gramps tapped his fingers on the chair again and gazed into space. "I got knocked out in the small room behind the loading dock, but I don't remember much about that. I don't remember anything about the guy in the bike accident, though."

He looked at Gabby to see if the information was helpful. Gabby gave Gramps a big smile and a big thumbs up. "Thanks, Gramps. That helps a lot! We know the treasure map is real, and now you have made us believe that the treasure hunt was real as well."

Carly reached over and patted Gramps' arm. "You are a big help, Gramps, and we love you." Jodie went over and gave Gramps a hug. Gramps teared up a bit at that.

"Strangely enough," Ernie told the group, "I remember something about that bike accident. It happened over by the golf course, sure. But more notably, it happened right in front of your grandfather Grant's house."

18

Marco

Just as Gabby guessed, Mom was not happy when they relayed Gramps' story about the two men rummaging through his things. As soon as supper was finished, she went over to the assisted living to get to the bottom of things. Papa John went along to calm things down. It was never a good idea to get on Mom's bad side, which was why Gabby thought they should back away from the idea of taking the map to the factory to see if they could follow the clues to the treasure. What they needed was access to someone who had worked at the factory in those days and could talk about that time.

Tim said he thought a good place to start was Sally's Sandwich Shop. Sally was a wealth of information about anything going on in Eagle River. A lot of the talk in this town passed through the doors of her restaurant every day. The kids planned to have lunch there tomorrow and hoped she would give them a name of someone who might have information about the treasure hunting days at the factory.

Right then, Gabby and Jodie were pedaling around town on a different kind of hunt. They weren't looking for treasure; they were looking for Marco. Marco was Olivia's younger brother, and Olivia was Tim's girlfriend. It was their uncle who had gone missing and was the focus of the Eagle River Detectives' last case.

Marco was in fifth grade, the same as Vivian. In fact, Gabby had seen Marco and Vivian gliding through town on more than one occasion. That might be a problem, but he had an idea he wanted to run by Marco.

The evening was pure wonder. The warm air caressed their faces as they slid through town, crisscrossing the blocks, hoping to spot the object of their quest. If you lived in this town, Marco had been ridden by your house whether you knew it or not. Marco nearly lived on his bicycle. He had become such a fixture in town that when he passed you by you gave it no thought. Marco loved this town and cruised its streets daily. That was why Gabby wanted to talk with him.

Gabby was pretty sure that he and Jodie, as well as Owen and Vivian, were being watched. Why would those men have known to search Gramps' room for clues unless they had followed the kids to Sumner House. Gabby was interested in that bicycle accident near Grandpa Grant's house, and who better to scout things out than Marco?

"There he goes." Eagle-eyed Jodie pointed to an intersection a block away. Marco was already out of sight, but they now knew where to look. Every block in this part of town had two or three streetlights which made the ride magical. It was dark, but not dark as you rode in and out of the lighted areas. Gabby loved this town.

The twins raced to the corner, hoping not to lose sight of Marco. He had a block and a half lead on them, but they sped up and began to close the gap. "Marco!" Jodie called out. Hearing his name, the boy slowed down and looked back. When he saw Gabby and Jodie he stopped and waited for them to catch up.

"Marco, just the man I wanted to see," Gabby greeted the boy with a high-five. Marco high-fived back with a big smile. Gabby knew Marco thought Tim was one of the coolest people to walk the earth and was hoping some of that hero worship would pass to him as Tim's brother.

Marco seemed to stand a little taller as he looked expectantly at Gabby. "Me?" he said. "You were looking for me? What can I do for you?" Jodie smiled at Marco. He was a cute kid and seemed happy to be the center of the twins' attention.

Gabby got right down to business. "We are on another case and need your help."

"My help? You need my help?" Marco looked surprised. "I'm not good at anything."

"Think about it, buddy." Gabby refused Marco's assessment of himself. "Who knows this town better than you? We need you to do some scouting for us. We have people watching us a lot of the time, and we don't want to tip them off that we are looking for something."

"What are you looking for?" Marco was catching Gabby's excitement.

"That's the problem. We don't know. We just know that someone hid something somewhere in this town, and we want to find it before the bad guys do." As soon as Gabby said it, it sounded stupid. *Someone hid something somewhere in this town? Well, that should be easy for you to find, Marco.* Sometimes he felt like a real idiot.

"Can I start over?" Gabby could see that Marco was ready to back out of the conversation. "The thing is, we do know there is a treasure. And we do have a few clues, but we need more information to solve the case."

"We know that people at Grant Manufacturing were looking for this treasure years ago, but the plant closed suddenly when Grandpa Grant died, and it was never found." Jodie filled in those details.

"We'd like you to scout out Grandpa Grant's property. It's the large brick house with about an acre of land on the west side of the road just past the golf course."

"I know where it is," Marco said quietly.

"Look for other buildings on the lot. Just drive by a few times and tell us what you see," Gabby finished.

Marco looked worried. "How can I find anything if I don't know what I'm looking for."

"Just tell us what you see. Take a picture if you can. We want to figure out why one of the searchers from back then went looking for the treasure at Grandfather's house."

Marco had one foot on the bike pedal and was bracing himself on the other leg, holding the bike upright as he pondered the request. "I can do that, I guess, but I don't think I'll find anything."

"Great. Thanks, Marco." Gabby finally relaxed. He hadn't been sure Marco was going to agree to the assignment. "Oh, and one more thing. Don't go anywhere near that house when you are riding with Vivian."

19

Sally's

Gabby was pretty sure everyone who lived in Eagle River had eaten at Sally's Sandwich Shop at one time or another. Sally was the first to know when someone new moved to town, or a new baby was born, or someone was in the hospital. The news of the town flowed in and out of the restaurant's door as freely as did her customers. The customers were the source of the news, of course, so where better to go to get the pulse of the town.

Mom had said that many of the factory workers made their way to Sally's for their lunch break, and there was no reason to believe that many of those same folks hadn't found their way to Sally's back during the time of the treasure hunt craze. And if there was a buzz about the treasure, this would be the place where people would talk about it.

The kids were seated at a round table just inside the door. They had placed their order on the way in and had their drinks in front of them. The tables were almost all filled up, and only a few booths remained open. Most of the folks who came to a small-town café already knew each other, and the hum of conversation blended with the background music. It almost felt like a family gathering. Handshakes and hugs and friendly greetings could be seen in every direction. Gabby couldn't see why people would want to live any place other than right here in Eagle River.

The food arrived, and as they began eating, Sally stopped by their table with a big smile. "Nice to see you, detectives." She gave Carly a wink. Sally was one of the people who hadn't been too sure the Grants should have moved back to Eagle River when they first came to town, but Carly and the kids had won her over on their first case when they cleared Dad's name. It meant a lot to have Sally's approval. Now the town accepted them with open arms.

This was the perfect opportunity to ask Sally some questions. "Sally, you know we always enjoy hearing about things that happened in town before we moved here. Especially things about Grant Manufacturing."

The kids had discussed this at length. How do you ask the question without getting the other person to be suspicious?

"Somebody told us that there was some mystery about a woman who fell down the office stairs and broke her leg. We're detectives and breaking your leg from a fall doesn't sound like a mystery to me." Gabby casually took a bite of his sandwich and looked at Sally as though he needed an explanation.

Sally looked thoughtful. Gabby could tell she was mulling over the question.

"Well, from talk at the tables that day, I guess nobody understood why she was up in the office in the first place, but she had claimed that someone pushed her, causing the fall," Sally said, thinking back to that time. "There was talk that one of the people from the factory had been in a bike accident out near your grandfather Grant's house, and he had claimed to be knocked over, too. I guess people thought that the coincidence didn't make sense. It was a mystery why those things happened to two people they knew only days apart."

"Do you think the bicycle guy was telling the truth?" Tim asked.

Sally looked around the busy restaurant. "Why don't you ask him yourself? That's Larry Diller right over there." She pointed to a man in a nearby booth. He was looking at his phone and seemed to be enjoying his meal. Giving the kids a friendly wave, Sally returned to the counter to help with the orders.

* * *

Gabby looked at the others, and at Tim's nod got up and walked over to the booth where Larry Diller was sitting. The man looked up startled when he found Gabby standing in front of him.

"Could I talk with you for a few minutes?" the boy asked. Gabby could tell that the man was surprised at the question.

"Sure thing." The man smiled at the boy. "You're one of Otto Grant's grandkids, aren't you? He sure did love you kids." Larry Diller looked over at the other kids and smiled at them. Making a waving motion with his hand, he beckoned them over to his table. Puzzled, the kids got up and slid onto the bench across from the man. "I was telling your brother how proud your grandfather was of you four kids."

"But he didn't know us. We never met him," Carly assured the mistaken man.

"How could he be proud of us if he never met us?" Tim needed things to make sense.

"Well, I used to work at the factory, sure, but your grandfather called on me a lot to manage things around his house, too. I took care of getting things repaired if something broke, made sure the grass got cut, kept the outbuildings in shape—things like that. I got to know your grandfather as a friend. And I know for a fact that whenever your mom sent newsy letters and pictures of you kids to your grandpa and grandma Bertram, the two of them would make a trip to the Grant's house and all four of them would pour over the news. They watched you grow up from little on. One time, your grandfather told me he prayed for each of you kids every night before going to sleep."

Gabby looked at his sisters, both of whom had tears in their eyes. *Grandfather and Grandmother Grant knew who they were? They loved us?* Gabby looked at Larry Diller and leaned into the man, giving him a big hug. "Thank you, thank you. No one ever told us that."

Carly got up and gave the man a hug, too, and Jodie and Tim followed. By this time, it seemed as though all the people in the restaurant were staring at the group. They must have overheard the conversation, because Gabby could tell that even some of them had tears in their eyes.

"I know how happy Otto Grant would have been to know that someday you kids would be living here right in his hometown." Gabby could see that Larry Diller's eyes were suspiciously wet, too. "Now, what can I do for you kids?" he asked kindly. "You must have had something in mind when you came over to the table." Looking directly at the youngest boy, he said, "And you must be Gabby. Your grandfather always got a big kick out of your mom's 'Gabby' stories."

Gabby felt the tears form in his eyes roll down his cheeks and drop to the floor.

20

Larry Diller

Larry Diller had turned out to be a gold mine of information. Conversation was lively around the supper table that evening. The kids, sometimes all talking at the same time, sometimes at a loss for words, described for Mom and Papa John what Larry Diller had told them about the grandparents getting together and sharing Mom's newsy letters. Jodie told them that Grandpa Grant's friend had said that they loved getting the pictures, too.

"He said they watched us grow up!" Tim said, still having a hard time picturing it. He had mourned the loss of not knowing Grandfather and Grandmother Grant for many years.

"It feels like, because they knew us, we didn't miss out completely," Carly said, trying to put her feelings into words.

Ball was circling the table, stopping to look at their faces as they spoke. It was as though he knew something big had happened and hadn't quite figured out if it was a good thing or a bad thing,

"I'm so glad to know that they got to know you all. I bragged you up, you know." Looking at Tim, she said softly. "I told your grandfather that you had the business gene like he and your dad both did. I think he hoped you would take over the factory one day. And he would be so proud of you, Carly. You refused to give up. You pushed through until you cleared your father's name. All of you did," she said proudly looking over her talented children. "Jodie, you had the cutest smile as a baby, and Gabby, well, you got into all sorts of antics. I'm thrilled to know that they got to know each one of you."

"Mom," Gabby said, meeting his mother's shining eyes across the table, "every night, Grandfather prayed for us."

Now mom's eyes filled with tears. As of that day, Gabby knew one thing for sure. Happy tears were a real thing.

After clearing the table and putting away the food, the group followed Gabby out to their detective's "office"—the picnic table in the backyard. Reassured that all was well, Ball weaved in and out of the group creating chaos as usual.

Michael was coming over in a few minutes and Gabby wanted him in on this discussion.

Ball suddenly went tearing around the corner of the house and they heard someone yell, "Ball, get down. Cut it out!"

"Michael's here," Jodie piped up as Ball came tearing back around the corner to fetch the ball by the backyard fence.

Michael came around the corner and took a seat by Carly. Ball dropped a ball at his feet and went to find a comfortable place to lie down. Now that that ritual was over, they could get to work. Gabby called the meeting to order. Carly told Michael the story they learned about their grandparents from Larry Diller. Michael moved closer to Carly and gave her quick hug as if to show that he saw how much this meant to her.

"That wasn't all Larry Diller had to say, and that's why we are having this meeting," Gabby explained to Michael.

Tim added, "He was pointed out to us by Sally as the guy who was in the bicycle accident during all the treasure hunting craze at the factory. He not only worked at the factory, but he also took care of Grandfather Grant's property."

"He told us that the hidden treasure thing was some rumor going around the factory, and he didn't think it was true," Gabby continued the story. "Contrary to what people thought, he wasn't treasure hunting that day. He was at the Grant property because Grandfather had asked him to check the electrical lines. Something wasn't right. The lights kept flickering on and off in the house. But as he approached the house that day, a car was backing hurriedly out of the Grant's driveway. It clipped his bike's front wheel catapulting him into the air."

Jodie looked at Michael and finished the story. "Larry Diller told us that one of the guys in the car looked back and saw him land hard. Instead of stopping to see if he was hurt, the driver sped up and drove off."

* * *

The next morning Gabby and Jodie ate a quick breakfast and hopped on their bikes to go look for Marco. The two cruised through the town for over an hour without seeing any sign of him. They did see a lot of their other friends, though. They stopped to talk with at least five of them and waved to about six more. Nebraska's state motto was "The Good Life," and after this morning's pleasant outing, Gabby couldn't agree more.

"Let's check for Marco at his house. I'm getting tired. How does he do this every day?" Jodie's face was red from the effort of the long ride—not to mention the temperature heating up. It was easily in the 90s, Gabby guessed.

They weren't in any hurry. They slowly pedaled the four blocks to the Herrara's house. The leafy trees on both sides of the street supplied shade, and the warm breeze on their faces was soothing. Gabby was mulling over Larry Diller's story. He said he'd gotten banged up badly in that bike accident. He broke his left arm and had a bad cut on his shoulder from landing hard on one of the bike's pedals. The doctor told him that it was a good thing he was wearing his bike helmet. His head had slammed the pavement hard but there was no head injury because of that helmet. Gabby started counting the injuries in this case. Besides Larry Diller, there was the woman who broke her leg falling down the office stairs, Gramps who got knocked out, and Tim who had fallen from the cut rope ladder. Whoever was behind all this wasn't afraid to hurt people that got in the way of their search.

As they rolled up the driveway, they saw Marco's bike leaning against the front porch. Olivia, Marco's sister, opened the door at their knock. Gabby smiled at her, and Jodie gave her a quick hug. Olivia was Tim's girlfriend, and the whole family loved this sweet-natured girl. "Hi, Olivia. We're looking for Marco. Is he home?"

"Haven't you heard?" Olivia's eyes were wide. "Marco's in the hospital."

* * *

Olivia's words landed on Gabby's brain like a hammer blow. He felt the blood drain from his face. He was as close to fainting as he could ever remember. Both Olivia and Jodie were looking at him with concern.

What were you thinking to involve a ten-year-old in this dangerous business? You are such an idiot! Gabby knew he had messed up big time and could hardly get the dreaded question out of his mouth. "What happened?" He couldn't even look at Olivia, he was so upset with himself and worried for Marco.

"He came home last night with a bad side ache, and when it didn't get better, Mom took him to the emergency room. He had an emergency appendectomy early this morning," Olivia explained. "Are you okay, Gabby?"

Gabby took two wobbly steps toward the porch swing and plopped on the swing in relief. "Oh, good!" he said as he gave a silent prayer of thanks that God had kept Marco safe.

"I don't know what's good about an emergency operation, but you look kind of sick yourself." Jodie couldn't figure out what had just happened.

"Mom called and said Marco is already feeling better. He needs to stay one night in the hospital, but he's coming home tomorrow," Olivia reassured the twins.

"That's great, Olivia. Tell him hi for us and that we are praying for a fast recovery." Gabby had made a fast recovery, too, now that he knew he was not responsible for putting Marco into the hospital. "Let's go, Jodie. Bye, Olivia."

"What was that about?" Jodie quizzed her twin.

Gabby was already pedaling down the driveway. "I'll tell you on the way home."

21

The Factory

Owen and Vivian weren't going to be back from their family vacation for a few more days, so Gabby thought this was probably as good a time as any to approach Mom about coming out to the factory to follow the steps of the treasure hunters from long ago. They had the same map the others had and would probably end up not finding the treasure just as the other's had not found the treasure, but they needed to try.

Carly was in the kitchen reading a magazine with a cup of tea at her side. She was the only one home. Gabby opened the refrigerator door out of habit and gazed blankly within. Carly didn't even look up from her article. "There are a couple of pieces of left-over chicken you can heat up in the microwave if you like, and a fresh salad in that big bowl in front. There is fresh bread on the counter, and raspberry jam on the second shelf." Their big sister didn't usually fix their lunch, but she made sure that there was something easy for the twins to prepare themselves.

"We're thinking of going to the plant to see if Mom is willing to let us follow the treasure map. You want to come?" Jodie loved it when the older siblings did things with them. Now that Tim had a job at the hardware store and Carly had taken over the household chores to free Mom up to run the plant, they weren't able to join the twins as often as they used to.

"Papa John said we should order out for pizza tonight since we haven't done that in a while, so supper is taken care of. I'm in the mood for a little detecting, so why not? Tim gets off at one o'clock today. How about we wait for him, and all go together?" Carly looked up from her magazine to smile at her little sis. A happy Jodie smiled right back.

* * *

Carly had her driver's license, but today she didn't have a car. Papa John's law office was only a few blocks from the house, and he would often walk to work so that Carly could have access to a car for running the household errands. Today he had business at a neighboring town, hence, no car. Michael and his car were their next means of transportation, but he had a dentist appointment that he had been trying to avoid. His mom had put her foot down and said that this time he was going.

That was fine with Gabby. He thought it was great to roll through the countryside on their bicycles, all four of them traveling together once again. This had been the Eagle River Detectives' only means of getting around on their first case. That seemed a long time ago to Gabby.

The Factory

Mom had agreed to the mystery map walk through but cautioned them about paying close attention to the safety rules. Factories were no place for carelessness. Mom must have alerted the entrance guard to their arrival, because he waived them right in. "Thanks, Jerry," Carly called out, and Jodie gave the smiling man a wave as they sped by.

They left their bikes in back by the loading dock and came in through the side entry. Tim had the rolled map tucked securely under his arm, and Carly had her ever-present notebook along to jot down their findings. Jodie led the way to Mom's office. Gabby had suggested they start there. Step two of the map directed the seeker to the office steps and the big window overlooking the factory. They could view the first site on the map from the window.

Mom was at her desk, talking on the phone. She mouthed a quick hello to the kids and went back to her conversation. Tim carefully unrolled the map, and they all compared it to what they could see out the window on to the factory floor below. To their left was the workstation on the map. The person working the big machine was no one they knew, but they recognized what he was making. Tim affirmed what the others had guessed. "He's putting together the frames for the Murphy beds. That's so cool." They loved the Murphy bed in the playhouse. It had a neat cover. When the bed was pushed up to the wall, the legs would fold in and when the bed was fitted into the framed box, you discovered that the bottom of the bed was covered with a large piece of wood with an elegant design. Carly made a note to ask Gramps if he remembered who used to work that machine.

The third spot on the map directed the searcher to the far-right side of the large window. The drawing of the dial was still there. There were numbers around the circular drawing. It looked something like a clock or a stopwatch. The center of the circle was empty. When you peered through the center it directed your eyes to one of the large beams that held up the factory roof. So far, there wasn't anything new that they hadn't guessed from studying the map at home.

Gabby gazed out the window. Were they missing something? He turned to the others and said, "I think we're done here. Let's go look at that post."

They waved goodbye to Mom who was still talking earnestly to whoever was on the other end of the phone call. As they trooped down the steps and over to the directed beam, Gabby experienced a letdown. *So far this treasure hunt is a real bust.* He wasn't sure if it was because there had been many others who had already followed the map and come up empty handed or if the map itself was uninspiring.

The post held three sets of numbers and letters. The first set, probably written with a permanent marker, said L17. Below that, another set read R28. Last of all, below that was L4. Obviously, the image on the window wasn't a watch face or a clock face. Gabby was pretty sure it didn't have anything to do with his compass dial, either. Tim was the first to get it. "That's the numbers for a combination lock. I have one on my locker at school. You turn the knob to the right until you get to the seventeenth notch, then go to the left until you get between the 25 and the 30 and stop at notch 27."

"And then go back to the right, past the zero and stop at the fourth notch." Jodie was pleased she could follow what Tim was saying. "It's like a secret language. It's easy once you know the key." She smiled at Gabby, thinking about their work on the secret code.

As happy as he was to have that part figured out, it was still a letdown. If they figured it out so quickly, he was pretty sure the other treasure hunters had reached the same conclusion. Looking back at the map, there was only one more clue.

Carly was looking intently at the drawing. "I guess we are looking for a door with a big handle. In the picture it has a padlock on it. At least we can get in to see whatever the door is hiding."

Tim said he didn't remember there being many closed doors in the factory. The vast building was mostly open floor space with various workstations visible throughout the building. The children started at one end of the room and made a giant circle around the space, making sure they hadn't overlooked anything. They found a total of four doors, but they all led outside the building, and none of them had the large handle in the picture on the map.

"The only places left are the bathrooms and the loading areas, and I've been to the bathroom, and it doesn't have that handle," Gabby told the group.

"The girls' doesn't either," added Jodie, just to make sure they covered all their bases.

Gabby led the way to the loading dock. You could get there from inside the building so that the workers could bring the finished furniture pieces to the trucks without having to deal with the weather. Gabby noted that it was raining softly as they rounded the corner to the docks. It was going to be a wet ride home. The docking area had plenty of doors, but they were garage doors, not the kind of door on the map. Turning so that their backs were to the large doors, they saw it. The door had a large handle, but the lock was gone.

* * *

Gabby reached for the handle and opened the door. This was their last hope of gaining anything of value from the once treasured map. Tim took the lead into the storeroom and the girls followed. Gabby paused before entering, preparing himself for the disappointment he was sure to find within.

The room held nine or ten pieces of furniture in various states of disrepair. Six or seven chairs were standing in a huddle in the right corner. Some had rips in the fabric, while others were missing backs or legs. Side tables with legs that didn't match stood next to couches with missing cushions. The letdown was obvious. Jodie was first to break the silence. "You know what this reminds me of? Santa's island of misfit toys."

Good old Jodie, Gabby thought as he laughed with the others. She always seemed to know just what to say to break the tension. The kids spent a little time looking around more carefully in case they missed something, but gaining access to this room hadn't helped the others who had set out so hopefully those many years ago, and there was nothing here for them either. If there was a treasure here, it was long gone. *Worst. Treasure. Hunt. Ever.*

22

Finding Marco

The rain slowed to a drizzle as they slogged home on their bikes. They rode side by side as much as possible since that prevented the wheels of their bikes from slinging water from the wet road onto the rider behind them. They mostly had the road to themselves at this time of day, so they were able to talk as they rode. Gabby asked if each of them could share their takeaway from the hunt. Yeah, just as he thought. *Worst treasure hunt ever.* After stowing their bikes on the porch to keep them out of rain and then retreated to their rooms to change into dry clothes. "I'm going to order the pizza in an hour, so let me know what you would like before then," Carly informed the group before they scattered.

Gabby was sitting glumly on the edge of his bed when Tim came into the bedroom, still toweling his wet hair from a shower. "What's up with Detective Gabby? Ready to give up after a little setback?"

"Yes. No. I guess not," Gabby stammered, "but the treasure map was our biggest clue up until now. I mean, where do we go from here? Maybe you and Carly need to take this one over."

"First of all, Carly and I don't mind being a part of the team, but neither of us has the time to 'take over' as you put it. We don't have a failed-to-solve case yet. I guess there is always a first time," Tim teased.

"The Eagle River Detectives do not fail to solve their cases." Gabby had his hands on his hips as he faced his brother with fire in his eyes. "Don't worry about it. I got this." With that he walked out the door and called for Jodie to hurry up if she wanted any say in the pizza order. He took the steps, two at a time, and tripped over Ball at the bottom of the stairs. He could hear Tim laughing as he got up. He brushed himself off and made up his mind right then and there. He was going to solve this case no matter what it took. Eagle River Detectives rule!

* * *

The next morning, Gabby and Jodie were back on their bikes rolling through town on the lookout for Marco. They had gone to his house first, not sure whether he was allowed to ride his bike so soon after surgery. Olivia had answered the door and told them that Marco had left on schedule to do his scouting rounds. Gabby wondered what Olivia meant by "scouting rounds" and intended to ask Marco the moment they found him.

It was another beautiful summer morning. Yesterday's rain had left the lawns greener and the grass longer. On every block a homeowner was already up and mowing the grass. The summer flowers had a fresh look to them. Gabby liked to think about how God could water the whole town in an hour's time with simple steady rain. While they were cruising through downtown, they saw Owen and Vivian up ahead. "Hey, Owen, Vivian, wait up," Gabby shouted as he and Jodie put on the speed to catch up.

Vivian signaled to Owen to hold up and wait for their friends. "We didn't know you were back from vacation." Jodie gave Vivian a hug. "How was it?"

"It was great to see our dad and nice to be somewhere where we weren't constantly being followed," Vivian answered. Gabby gave Owen a fist bump greeting. He had almost forgotten. Figuring out why those men were following these kids around was what got them involved in the mystery in the first place. They had to break this case just so those men would leave their new friends alone.

"We're on our way to the park," Owen said. "Want to come?"

"Sure," Gabby answered. They could look for Marco later.

* * *

Owen and Vivian's mom wanted them home for lunch, so Gabby and Jodie went home briefly, too. They ate sandwiches and had a glass of milk, grabbed a couple of cookies, and headed back to their search for Marco. After fifteen minutes of riding around with no sign of the boy, Gabby suggested they go to his house and ask Olivia where he might be.

They found Vivian with a slightly worried look on her face. "It's funny you should ask. My mom and I were just wondering where Marco was, too. He rides around town a lot of the day, but he always comes home for lunch. It's one of Mom's rules."

"We haven't been looking long," Gabby reassured the girl. "We'll keep looking and tell him to head home when we find him." They waved a cheery goodbye and rolled down the driveway to resume their search.

After a half hour of no luck, Gabby began to worry. He knew where he had to look next, but should he take Jodie with him? Maybe if she could stay hidden, she wouldn't be in any danger but could go for help if things turned bad. He told her of his suspicions and of his plan to use her as a lookout. Being Jodie, she agreed to do whatever would help the most. For about the hundredth time, he wondered how other people got through life without having a twin!

Grandpa Grant's former house was at the edge of town by the golf course. He had seen it numerous times in the past two years, but now he knew that Gramps and Grandma Bertram had often driven over to this house to bring the letters and pictures that Mom had sent, and he wanted to picture them driving into the driveway with the eager Grants out on the porch waiting for the news. *They loved us.* He still could scarcely take it in.

No one was living in the house at present. That meant they didn't have to worry about someone coming out of the house to yell at them, but it also meant that the neighbors knew there shouldn't be any activity around the house and yard. People in small towns were known for their willingness to look out for their neighbors' property. They would need to be careful.

Before rounding the final corner to Grandpa Grant's street, Jodie waved at her brother to stop. They tucked themselves and their bikes behind a bushy shrub at the corner and peered at the house from cover. What they saw was alarming. A black car was backing out of Grandpa Grant's driveway. The driver was in a hurry and drove quickly past the hidden bikers. There were two men in the front seats. The car went by so quickly they couldn't tell if there was a little kid in back or not.

* * *

The car was long out of sight when the two sleuths rolled slowly past the house. Nothing stirred. Even the birds were silent. Making a U-turn, the twins pedaled past the closed-up house from the other direction. There was a row of bushes along the sidewalk shielding the backyard from view. Gabby motioned Jodie to turn into the yard and let the bushes shield *them* from view instead.

Leaving their bikes behind the shrubbery, they surveyed the yard. The garage was not attached to the house but set back in the yard at the end of a long driveway. There was a basketball hoop next to the wide paved area extending out from the garage. Gabby tried to picture his dad shooting lay-ups and three pointers from the court-like area. The yard was large, and in the very back was a shed that Gabby had not noticed before. "You're sure this is the most likely place to find Marco?" Jodie looked at Gabby skeptically.

Gabby gave a big sigh. "It's my fault Marco is missing and may be in danger. I asked him to scout out the house for us because we thought it was too dangerous for us to do it. Pretty stupid, huh? No real detective would send a kid to do the dangerous work on a case." Gabby was still disgusted with himself.

"I think you're being too hard on yourself, Gabby. Marco agreed to do it, so let's get back to finding him." Jodie was a no-nonsense sort of kid.

The shed seemed the obvious place to start. The door was locked of course, but it was secured by an all too familiar gadget—a combination padlock. The twins looked at one another with delight. *Maybe that stupid treasure map was good for something after all.* "L17, R28, L4." They shouted in unison!

"Is somebody out there?" They heard the question coming from inside the building.

"Is that you, Marco?" Gabby asked with a hope-filled heart.

"Yeah, it's me. Marco. Can you get me out? I'm hungry."

* * *

As they suspected, the combination worked on the lock, and they had the door open in no time. "Thanks," said a grateful Marco as he bolted to retrieve his hidden bike. "I've got to get home. See ya!" And with a backward wave of his hand high in the air, he sped off.

"What just happened there?" Jodie was the first to break the stunned silence. "I mean, 'Thank you. I have to go home?' That's it? How long was he locked up in there? How did he get locked up in there?"

It didn't happen that often, but, as Gabby watched Marco disappear, he had nothing to say. There were simply had no words to explain that crazy turn of events.

23

Marco Rocks!

The next morning, Gabby and Jodie were on their bikes on the lookout for Marco. There was no way Gabby was going to continue the investigation without some explanation from Marco. This time they spotted him coasting past the library and caught up with him on the next block.

"Hi, guys." Marco seemed his usual friendly self. "I was just headed toward your house to give you my scouting report. You were right to be suspicious about the old Grant place. My sources claim there has been activity around that shed in the backyard for the past week or so. That's why I was there to check it out."

"How did you get locked into the building?" Jodie really wanted to know. Marco was still unconcerned about that little detail.

"Oh, that." Marco seemed a little embarrassed. "I made a miscalculation. Yesterday, one of my block lieutenants told me that those two men had been in the shed that morning.

I told her I would check it out. That's why I wasn't too worried about getting out. She knew where I was going and that I would check back in with her that afternoon. When I didn't show up, she would have come looking for me.

"What I didn't realize, though, was that they were men in there when I went in. Fortunately, I saw them before they saw me, and was able to hide behind some old boxes. When they left, they locked me in." Marco looked at Jodie to see if she was satisfied with his very logical explanation.

Gabby wasn't ready to move on just yet. "One of your 'block lieutenants'? What do you mean?"

"Oh, that. Well, as you know I have been patrolling this town for several years now. I see it as my duty to report anything that seems not right, like those guys on your grandpa's old property. Over time I have recruited assistants. My goal is one good outlook on every square block. I have about twenty lieutenants now, and between us, we keep things in pretty good order if I have to say so myself." Marco stood up straight and puffed out his chest a bit.

Gabby's mouth fell open in astonishment. *Marco was a one-man security force for the folks who lived in Eagle River? Who does that?"*

Jodie was buying it totally. "That's awesome, Marco. How do you find your block lieutenants?"

"Oh, that." Marco said. "It's easy. I just ask the people I run into from day to day who is the nosiest person in their neighborhood. Then I start bringing that person, most often an elderly lady, pieces of news that I have picked up here and there, and after we become friends, I ask if they want to be a block lieutenant, and they almost always say yes. Easy-peasy."

Brilliant. Gabby was in awe of the information network this quiet little kid must have developed over the past two years. "Marco, what would you say if you were asked to come to one of the Eagle River Detectives meetings?"

"I'd say yes!" said a wide-eyed Marco.

* * *

Gabby called an emergency meeting for that very day. They were meeting right after the evening meal so Marco could come before it turned dark. Michael couldn't be there, but the others were sitting in the backyard at the picnic table. Gabby had filled the group in on the amazing boy, so when Marco rounded the corner of the house with Ball at his heels, he got a warm reception from the group. He seemed pleased, but uncomfortable with all the attention. That made sense to Gabby. Marco's superpower was his ability to *not* be noticed.

The investigation had stalled out, and Gabby was hoping Marco could give them some solid leads. "Let's start the meeting by letting Marco tell us what he discovered yesterday." Gabby was eager to get back to the case.

"Well, when Gabby and Jodie asked me to check out the old Otto Grant property, I was willing, but nothing had crossed my attention up until then. I was surprised when one of my block lieutenants said she had been concerned about two men who were seen more than once on the property. Before I could get any more information, I ended up in the hospital and had surgery. It was three or four days before I was back on my rounds, but because I had asked about the house, my block watchers paid special attention to the place and had seen the men on the property at least once every day since I had asked."

"Were they trying to get into the house or the garage?" Tim asked.

"Not that we could tell," Marco answered cautiously. "What they did do was enter the shed in back and spend about an hour there every day. Because of that report, I expected them to be gone by the time I entered the building. But after I hid, I could hear them talking in a different language. It sounded like they were talking to someone not in the building. I could hear what they said, but not the answers from the person they were talking to. I guessed they were on the phone."

Carly was intrigued. "Could you make out anything they were saying?"

"I heard 'Grant Manufacturing,' but the rest was in their language. After I was locked in, I had a chance to look around. They hadn't been on their cell. They were using an old-fashioned ham radio set up in the shed for their communications."

"What's a ham radio?" Jodie looked confused.

"I had to do a little research on that topic myself." Marco let Jodie know this was not something that everyone knew about. "It's a way to call anywhere in the world on a private channel, and unless someone knows what channel you are using, there is no way to trace the call."

24

Gramps and Ernie

The next day was Wednesday. That meant an afternoon visit to Gramps and Ernie. Both Michael and Carly were free to come, so as soon as Tim got off work, they set out for Sumner Place. Michael offered to drive, but Gabby wanted to walk. Gramp's residence was eight blocks away, and Gabby wanted to talk as they walked. They needed to take advantage of this visit by asking some key questions. Carly had her pad and pen at the ready to capture anything they might want to bring up while they had Gramps and Ernie's attention.

Tim said he was still curious why Gramps was going into the room of misfit furniture where he claimed to have been knocked out. Michael wanted to know what the shed in their grandpa Grant's backyard had been used for when their grandfather owned the place. Carly was concerned about Gramps and wanted to know if the two men had been spotted near Sumner Place again since searching Gramps' room. Jodie reminded everyone that they wanted to ask

Gramps who had once worked on the machine that made the Murphy bed frames.

"And I want to ask Ernie if he remembers any Federal interest in town at the time of the treasure hunt at the factory," finished Gabby.

The two men were sunning on the back patio as usual. After hugs all around, the kids went to work with their questions. Gramps said he was in the damaged goods room to take notes on the needed repairs. "Now that I think back on it, I was there for another reason. There was a perfectly good Murphy bed in that room that your grandfather Grant and I decided would be a great addition to the playhouse we were building. I wanted to take some measurements. The carpenters planned to install it that week and wanted more information on the size." Gramps was pleased to remember that detail. Gabby was disappointed that there was no clear reason Gramps got attacked.

The shed in Grandfather Grant's backyard was mostly for garden equipment. At one time, Albert Decker had a mini workshop set up in the back. He was always a tinkerer, and while it was known that the inventor sometimes did jobs for one of the government agencies, Gramps had no idea what he did for them. Ernie assured the group that there had been no more intruders. The staff had been very upset to hear that the men had breached their security system and had been extra vigilant since the incident.

Gramps thought it was Albert Decker who had once worked on the machine shown on the map. "He was absolutely brilliant at his designs for the wooden covers," Gramps said in fond remembrance.

And finally, Ernie had what seemed like the most helpful answer to their questions. "I hadn't really tied those things together because I didn't know about the treasure hunt at the factory, but at about that time, two FBI agents came asking if I had noticed any foreigners about town. It was an odd question, I thought, but I told them no and put it out of my mind."

Satisfied that all their questions had been answered, the conversation turned to other things, like Tim's job, the twins' friendship with Owen and Vivian, and Carly's discovery of a hidden box of Grandma Bertram's cookie recipes. Ernie got a big kick out of Marco's network of nosey grandmas, but when Gabby told him about the ham radio set-up, he became alarmed.

"You know who are the biggest users of that technology?" he asked. "Spies."

* * *

On the way home, the Eagles River Detectives had a lot of information to mull over. The idea that the men who had been following Owen and Vivian could be spies seemed likelyas far as Gabby was concerned. It fit. The foreign language, the ham radio, the knowledge that Owen and Vivian's grandfather was an inventor who sometimes worked for the government, all supported the theory that there were foreign spies involved.

"Okay. Let's assume that these men are looking for something that is important enough for them to remain in the area—maybe even illegally," Tim observed. "What are they looking for?"

"So much of this is tied to the treasure hunt, long ago," Michael noted. "Why does that matter?"

"Albert Decker was working on the machine pictured on the map. Owen and Vivian are being followed, and their grandfather was Albert Decker," Gabby pointed out. Albert Decker must be the key.

* * *

That night, as they were finishing the evening meal, Mom mentioned that she had received a call from Lila Sampson, asking if the two of them could get together. They were meeting for coffee after work the next day. Gabby was happy to hear that. He was convinced that Albert Decker was an important piece of this mystery, and they needed to figure out how he fit in to the puzzle.

He and Jodie had talked at breakfast and decided the best way to start would be to talk with Larry Diller. As Jodie pointed out, both he and Albert Decker were working at the factory at the time of the treasure map incident. "Larry Diller told us all about Grandfather Grant, maybe he can fill us in on Owen's grandpa as well." Jodie came up with some good stuff.

They were on their way to Sally's, hoping Larry Diller was following his usual pattern of eating his noon meal there. Spotting the man they were looking for, they put in an order for sandwiches and drinks and walked over to his table as they waited for their food. Larry Diller saw them approaching and gave them a welcoming smile.

"Hi, kids," he greeted them warmly. "What can I do for you?"

Gabby was not surprised by the kindness of this man, but he was always warmed by the feeling of acceptance they now experienced in this little town. Once the townspeople decided you were one of them, they treated you as if you belonged: as if you were a member of a big, friendly family.

"Hi, Mr. Diller. Thanks again for telling us about Grandfather Grant. We were hoping you could tell us something about Albert Decker. He is the grandpa of our new friends, Owen and Vivian Sampson," Gabby was the first to speak, as usual.

"Albert Decker, huh?" Larry Diller tilted his head in thought. "I heard that Lila was back in town. What did you want to know?"

"You mentioned that Albert Decker sometimes used the shed on Grandpa Grant's property as a workshop. Do you know what he was working on?" Jodie could picture the shed but couldn't imagine what kind of project Albert Decker would be doing there.

Larry Diller slowly shook his head from side to side. "No, I don't believe I heard much about it. I do remember it was pretty hush-hush at the time. People knew he didn't want to talk about it, so they didn't ask."

"Did he have any close friends that might know more?" Gabby was grabbing at straws. Any lead would do.

Nodding a thoughtful yes, Larry Diller gave them a name. "George Evans worked the machine right next to him. Those two were real buddies. George lives at your grandpa's new home, Sumner Place. Maybe you could get your questions answered there."

A lead! Gabby gave a mental fist pump and thanked the kind man in front of them. As he and Jodie went to pick up their order, Gabby said a quick prayer, thanking God for giving them the gift of being a part of Eagle River and for the joy of getting to know the people who lived there.

* * *

That night at the evening meal, Mom told the group about her meeting with Lila Decker Sampson. She said they had a good time reminiscing about High School and their cheerleading days. Jodie tried to get Mom to show them one of her cheers, but Mom laughingly refused, saying that it would lose its effect when done by one person. Her face was getting red, and Gabby knew she was embarrassed by the idea, so he chimed in as well, begging her to show them at least one cheer routine. Carly offered to partner up with Mom since she was now a cheerleader and could easily follow Mom's moves. It was fun to tease her.

Papa John finally came to her rescue and said that she should stick to her decision because he wasn't sure he wanted to see her fall on her face, which made Mom defend herself. "I could do it if I wanted to, you know," she told Papa John. She was standing, hands on hips, giving her husband an outraged look. Gabby thought she was magnificent. The whole scene made everyone roar with laughter. Mom lost her fire when she realized Papa John was teasing, and she dissolved into laughter with the rest.

When things finally calmed down, Mom got back to her report. Lila Sampson had told Mom that her father, Albert Decker, had died several years ago. During the last few weeks of his life, he was surrounded by his family and was able to interact with them off and on. He was weak, and slept a lot, but on the occasions when he was awake, the family looked at picture albums and talked about happy times in the past. Albert was too weak to talk, but he still understood and enjoyed the stories that she and her mom and sisters told.

The one exception was when Lila shared the picture of the cheerleader's party at the playhouse. When he looked at the picture, her father's eyes widened, and he became agitated. Lila's mom had no explanation for the reaction, so they put the picture away, gave him some medication to help him calm down, and let him sleep. The next day, he seemed to have forgotten the incident, so they stayed away from the topic and things went back to the way they had been. Now, though, Lila was curious to see if she could figure out what might have caused that reaction. She wondered if Mom would mind letting her visit the playhouse once again. They were meeting at the factory on Friday afternoon and would go to examine it together.

Gabby asked if he, Jodie, Owen and Vivian could come, too. The friends were meeting at the park for a picnic lunch that day and could ride over on their bikes later in the afternoon. Mom couldn't see any problem with that, so that was settled.

That night, Gabby said his bedtimes prayers, thanking God for his fun family and for friends and Gramps and Ernie, and for his little town of Eagle River, Nebraska. "And keep us safe. In Jesus' name I pray, amen," whispered the tired boy. *Spies, huh?* He might not be the smartest detective in the group, but he was determined to figure this one out. Tomorrow, they would go to Sumner Place to see Ernie and Gramps. Gabby was hoping that Gramps remembered George Evans, the man who was a good friend of Albert Decker. He would really like to talk with that man. Maybe they could sit down with Carly and get a list of questions before they went. Satisfied that the Eagle River Detectives now had a new important lead, he gave a big yawn and fell asleep.

25

A Talk with George Evans

Armed with their list of questions, the three detectives rode their bikes to Sumner Place for the second time in two days. Carly had already made plans to go shopping with one of her friends from school, but Tim had a day off and offered to go with the twins. He told Gabby that he, too, was curious to meet someone who not only worked at Grant Manufacturing at the time of the treasure hunt excitement but who knew the mysterious Albert Decker as well.

Mom had called ahead to the folks at Sumner Place to let them know the kids would be visiting, so they went around to the back patio and found both Gramps and Ernie waiting for them. After the usual greetings and hugs, the kids brought over some chairs and got right down to business.

"Gramps, do you remember George Evans?" Gabby asked the opening question.

"Of course, I know George. We went to high school together. Grade school, too, for that matter. He lives right here on the second floor like I do." Gramps was smiling as he spoke. "George is a real character. When we were kids, he thought up all sorts of mischief, and the rest of us were dumb enough to go along with it. We would usually get in trouble, but he rarely did. You would think we would have figured that out, but we didn't."

Gabby felt a smile appear on his own face as Gramps talked with obvious enjoyment about his antics with George, the mischief maker.

"Was he still a prankster when he worked at the plant?" Jodie's eyes sparkled with delight at Gramps' George stories. She especially liked the one where he talked a nine-year-old Gramps into getting into a boxcar with him on a parked train at the train station. Before they knew it, the train started moving and they couldn't get back off until the next stop. The two little boys had a four mile walk to get back home.

"Do you think we could ask him some questions?" Tim asked Gramps. "We are interested in learning more about Albert Decker, and someone said that George and Albert were good friends.

"I'm sure George would enjoy a visit. He doesn't have a lot of family living nearby, so company is always welcome. He's usually sitting in the downstairs lounge. Let's go looking for him." Gramps was already moving toward the back door of the building, obviously eager to introduce his grandchildren to his mischievous childhood friend.

Gramps, Ernie, and the kids trooped through the lobby to the lounge. Sure enough. George was there just as Gramps had guessed. Seeing that the group was headed his way, George waved them over with a grin. "Who have you got here, Billy boy? Are these the Eagle River Detectives I've been hearing about?" Turning to the kids he added, "You're pretty famous in this town you know."

Gramps had a pleased look on his face. "George, meet three of my grandchildren, Tim, Gabby, and Jodie. They are interested in asking you a few questions. Do you mind?"

"Not at all. How can I help?" George looked at Gabby expectantly, since Gabby had stepped forward to pose the first query. "The reason we are here is that we have two new friends, and their grandfather was Albert Decker."

George's expression changed from cheerful to sad. "Ah, Albert. Yes, he and I were good friends until I went and messed things up. He was a brilliant physicist, and he would confide in me sometimes—not like what he was working on, of course. That was top secret. But he would tell me when he had breakthroughs, or how he always had to be careful that others did not get hold of his studies. I used to make jokes about his little secrets."

"It sounds like you really liked him." Jodie said. "We like Owen and Vivian, too. How did you mess things up?"

"Well, I like to tease folks, so just to get his goat, I drew this stupid treasure map."

"You drew the treasure map?" Tim looked stunned.

"You know about it, too? It was just a joke. I thought it was funny. Albert did not. To make matters worse, someone found the map and thought it was the real deal and all sorts of crazy things began to happen as people began to search for the treasure." George shook his head from side to side as if trying to figure out how a simple prank turned in to disaster that had cost him his friendship with Albert. "It was just a dumb map."

"We know," Gabby said under his breath. "Worst treasure map ever."

* * *

George had gone on to say that Albert had left town for a month or two to work further on his project with the government. When it was time to move back, Grandpa Grant had died, and the factory was closed. He felt bad that he never got to apologize properly. "I heard that Albert died a few years ago, and that Lila is back in town. If I ever see her, I'm going to tell her how sorry I was to lose her dad's trust."

The kids and Gramps and Ernie said goodbye to George. Gabby thanked him for answering their questions, and Jodie gave George a hug and promised they would stop to see him the next time they came to visit. That cheered George up, and he had a big smile back on his face as they turned to go.

"Did you draw that stuff on the other side of the map, too?" Tim slipped in one last question. He wanted to clear up the whole map thing before leaving.

"I don't know why I did that. I never wanted to see that map again. It just reminded me how foolish I had been to risk losing a great friendship. But I overheard some guys talking about the treasure. They said they had an idea where the treasure was hidden, so I added the clue to the map."

"You drew kids playing ball and a house. What kind of clue was that?" Jodie asked. She was still frustrated that the map made no sense.

"Pretty simple if you ask me." George had tired of talk about the map. "The guy with the new clue said 'playhouse.'"

26

What Next?

When the kids got back to the house, they found Carly and Michael sitting on the porch swing. They had talked among themselves on the ride back from Sumner Place and now brought the other two up to date.

"You mean all the craziness surrounding the treasure map happened because of some prank?" Carly was stunned by the news. She opened her ever present notebook. "This changes everything. We need to make a list of what we know to be true and what may not be true if the map is a fake." She drew a line down the page and wrote *True* on one side and *Not true* on the other.

"The treasure map may be fake, but I think there is still a lot of evidence that there is a treasure." Gabby began to list the reasons: "For one thing, the foreign spies are still in town snooping around and keeping tabs on Owen and Vivian. Number two, we know Albert Decker was worried about keeping his work for the government a secret, and thirdly, someone tried to discourage us from continuing this investigation by cutting the treehouse rope."

"Don't forget about the men using the shed to communicate by ham radio," Jodie piped in.

"And somebody trashed the playhouse," added Tim.

Carly was writing furiously. Michael looked over his girlfriend's shoulder to read the lists. "It's pretty obvious from what we have uncovered up to now is that the only thing we got wrong was thinking the treasure map would lead us to the treasure."

"Silly us," Gabby said sarcastically. "Where do we go from here?"

"We still have one mystery to clear up," Jodie reminded the group. "What does this have to do with the playhouse?"

* * *

The next morning, Gabby and Jodie biked through town looking for Marco. They needed an update on the strange men's whereabouts. Eventually, they spotted his bike in the bike rack at the library.

"Hi, kids! What can I help you with today?" Gabby enjoyed going to the library, mostly because of the town's flamboyant librarian, Ms. Cook. Today she was wearing orange stretch pants with a wildly flowered tunic. Her welcome still echoed through the building. Ms. Cook was cheerful, friendly, and loud.

"Hi, Ms. Cook. We're just looking for Marco," Gabby responded as his eyes swept the room for signs of their friend.

"He's in the science section looking up information on ham radios." Ms. Cook liked knowing everything about everyone.

"It's hard doing any sleuthing in this library," Jodie whispered the obvious to Gabby as they headed to the science section to find their friend. Marco looked up and smiled at the twins as he saw them approaching. "If you came looking for me, I assume Ms. Cook told you where I was," he said cheerfully. "She's one of my best block lieutenants, you know."

Brilliant. Once again, Gabby was blown away by this little kid's savvy. "Did you find anything useful about ham radios?"

"She told you that, too? Like I said, one of my best." Marco didn't seem to mind having Ms. Cook having so much information concerning his whereabouts. "I'm not looking for anything in particular. I thought it could be important to understand how this type of communication works. It might be something the Eagle River Detectives should consider. It's an interesting way of keeping in touch." Marco's enthusiasm was amazing.

"We found out who drew the treasure map, and it was a fake. It was a meant as a joke," Jodie filled Marco in on their visit with George Evans.

"Well," Marco said as he processed the new information, "The men are real, and they have been going to the shed every day now for the past week."

* * *

What Next?

As they pedaled home, Gabby shared his thoughts about Marco. "That kid is amazing. We should seriously consider asking him to become an Eagle River Detective. Michael is a member. There is nothing that says you must be a Grant to be part of the team."

"Exactly. You only need to be a part of Eagle River, and Marco is about as invested in this town as anybody else we know." Jodie liked the idea a lot.

27

Chasing Down the Final Clue

It was Friday morning. Gabby and Jodie were on their way to meet Owen and Vivian at the park. They had packed sandwiches, chips, and an apple for dessert. It was going to be a hot day. Just the short trip to the park had them both feeling the humidity. Their clothes stuck to their bodies as they pedaled. People were in their yards, getting the outdoor chores done before the real heat set in, this one weeding, that one cutting the grass, and another gathering produce from the garden. The sweet swell of summer flowers wafted in the air and a slight haze rose from the ground in the distance. Gabby loved this little town. The warm air brushed over his face as he turned into the park.

Owen and Vivian had found a great picnic table near the river and waved as they saw the twins coming. They fished for a while, becoming quickly bored when it became obvious the fish weren't biting. They worked on the code for a bit, each making a key using the simple form. Start with alphabet forward, write the key below using the letters backward. When done it looked like this:

A B C D E F G H I J K L M N O P Q R S T U V W X Y Z
Z Y X W V U T S R Q P O N M L K J I H G F E D C B A

They folded the papers into their pockets. Now they were ready, at a moment's notice, to use the code if needed. They laughed at their silliness, but, after all, detectives had to be prepared.

After eating their lunches, they packed up and headed for their bikes. They had an appointment to meet their mothers at the factory. They were going to the playhouse to see if anything Ms. Sampson saw could account for her father's reaction to the picture of the party she had attended there so many years ago.

The air had a notable stillness. Gabby had lived in this part of the country long enough to sense that a storm might be brewing, but for right now, it was hot and muggy and as they passed the cornfields it seemed as though they could watch the corn grow. It towered over their heads at this point of the summer, and everywhere he looked he saw green: row after row of tall, leafy plants, as far as the eyes could see. *Bumper crop.* He learned in social studies last year that Nebraska was the third largest producer of corn in the United States, bested only by number one, Iowa, and number two, Illinois.

The kids had become such familiar figures by now that the guard gave them a smiling wave through as they neared the factory gatehouse. Parking their bikes on the side where they wouldn't be in the way, the kids went in the side door,

Gabby in the lead. Owen and Vivian had never been to the factory before, so Gabby pointed out the various places indicated on the notoriously useless treasure map, including the machine Owen and Vivian's grandfather used to operate. Jodie led the way to the stairs, and the kids climbed to the office, expecting to see their moms waiting for them there.

The office was empty. The whole factory was eerily silent. Gabby wasn't too worried about that. On slow weeks, Mom often scheduled an early close of the workday on Fridays. But he was worried that their mothers hadn't waited for them."

"Do you think they forgot we were coming?" Jodie asked her brother. "It doesn't look as though she left us a note or anything."

"What's that on the floor?" Vivian was a noticer. "Is that the note, and it blew off the desk or something?"

"Gabby bent down and snagged the paper. "It's Mom's handwriting alright. It says '*Playhouse—HELP*'."

* * *

Owen turned toward the office door. "Let's go."

"Not so fast, guys," Gabby held out his hand indicating they should hold up. "We can't go barging into what might be a bad situation for our moms without a plan."

"I think those men came in here and forced them to take them to the playhouse." Jodie was almost crying at that point.

Gabby was silent for a moment as he said a quick prayer asking for God's help. As he finished, he looked down and spotted his mother's cell phone on the desk. "I've got an idea. I'm going to stay here and make a few calls. You three very carefully check out the playhouse, but make sure no one in that playhouse sees you. Don't do anything until I get there. I only need a few minutes."

Owen led the girls down the steps, and Gabby got to work. He called Tim and explained his plan. Tim agreed to help and hung up so Gabby could join the others. He needed to assess the situation firsthand. He found Owen peering carefully into one of the playhouse windows. The curtain was hanging off to the side, leaving a thin slit to see through. Owen stepped back and let Gabby stand in front of him. Gabby could see into the room, and what he saw was alarming. Mom and Ms. Sampson were sitting at the table. It appeared that their arms were taped to the arms of the chairs. He was relieved to see that they did not appear hurt, just immobilized. He couldn't see the men, but he could hear faint talking and it sounded as though there were at least two of them. They were on the far side of the room, opposite the door to the cabin. After a quick consultation, the group decided they would enter the little house as though they were expected.

The door was locked from the inside, but Gabby knew that Carly had hidden an extra key under the flowerpot on the windowsill in case they forgot to bring a key, *or in case they needed to rescue Mom and her friend,* he added.

Jodie had a sure and steady hand, so Gabby gave her the key. She slid it silently into the keyhole and turned it slowly. Just at the last twist, the mechanism gave a loud click, but by then Gabby had opened the door and the kids marched in.

"What's up, Mom?" Gabby pointed to the two men. *there were only two.* "What are they doing here, and why are you tied up?"

Mom's eyes were wide with surprise. Gabby guessed the last thing she expected was to see the four of them come in that locked door.

"You kids, beat it. This is grown up business." One of the men took a menacing step toward Gabby.

"Oh," quick-witted Jodie piped on, "you mean go for help?"

The two men exchanged exasperated looks. "Just stay out of the way then."

As Gabby looked around the cabin, he saw what had been right in their faces all the time. He knew what Albert Decker had seen in that picture. He eased his code out of his pocket. "We'll go sit over here," he waved vaguely at the couch in the living room. Writing on the bottom of his slip he tore a piece off and passed it to Jodie:

It said:

HRG LN YVW
KOZB XZIWH

The men had turned their attention back to the women.

Jodie took the first line: SIT ON BED

Vivian decoded the second: PLAY CARDS

One of the men glanced over and saw Jodie holding the note. He grabbed the note out of her hand. "What does this say?" he demanded looking at the gibberish.

"It's a code they use to talk to each other. I know how to break the code," Owen bragged to the man.

Meanwhile, Jodie and Vivian grabbed the strap and lowered the Murphy bed. Jodie grabbed a deck of cards from the game shelf, and the girls climbed up on the bed and began to play a game of UNO.

Gabby glared at Owen. *Don't you do it,* his eyes said.

"It says, 'Do exactly what these men tell you to do.'" Owen pretended to read the note.

"Okay. Smart kid." The man seemed satisfied.

Before the men could restart their questioning, the door opened again, and Tim came in along with Olivia, Marco, and Ball. Ball took a quick assessment of the room and at once stationed himself between the two men and the two women.

Tim and Olivia went over to the table and calmly began to remove the tape from the women's arms. Anytime one of the men moved or tried to speak, Ball would bare his teeth and give an ominous growl. Gabby could see sweat beginning to form on their foreheads.

At the knock on the door, Marco opened it for Papa John to enter. "What on earth is going on here?" The lawyer was visibly angry. "You tied them up?" he asked incredulously. "That is grounds for kidnaping."

"Papa John should know. He is a lawyer after all," Gabby whispered to wide-eyed Marco.

"I'm calling the police right now," continued the irate husband.

"No need," Gabby told his stepdad as the door opened and in walked the new sheriff in town. The kids still called him Uncle Brian, since that is how he was introduced to them by Carly's friend, Jeff, when they had first moved to Eagle River.

Speaking of Carly, she and Michael opened the door and squeezed past the sheriff into the crowded room. "It looks as though justice is about to be served," Michael noted.

"Hi, Uncle Brian," Carly said as she crossed the room to give her mom a big hug.

By this time, Vivian was sitting contentedly on her mom's lap, and Owen was standing protectively at her side. Ball was on full alert, and the sheriff was pulling out a pair of handcuffs.

"This is awesome," said Marco.

28

The Playhouse

As the sheriff and Papa John went out the playhouse door, leading the now handcuffed men to the sheriff's car, Gramps and Ernie came in the playhouse door. "Did we miss something?" Gramps seemed disappointed as he watched the sheriff's car pull out of the driveway.

"You missed the part about trapping the spies in the playhouse." Jodie could laugh about it now. "When we decided to rescue Mom and Ms. Sampson, Gabby told us he didn't think we could overpower them, but he was pretty sure we could outnumber them!"

At this, the whole group laughed and began high fiving and backslapping in celebration. Ball barked his agreement as well. The plan had worked very well, indeed, and Gabby could see they were all pleased to have been in on it!

"But you didn't miss everything," Gabby assured Gramps and Ernie. "The best part is still to come. I know where the treasure is!" All eyes turned to Gabby. "And I know why Albert Decker was so upset with his friend, George."

Jodie asked the question they were all thinking. "Why?"

"Because the map was real. It really did lead to the treasure, but what no one knew was that the treasure had been moved! It's right here in the playhouse."

He turned to Ms. Sampson. "As soon as we walked in the door today, I saw what your father had seen in that picture you showed him. "Tim, could you put the Murphy bed into its case?" Gabby nodded toward the bed.

Tim walked to the foot of the bed and found the strap used to lift the mattress toward the wall were the case stood.

As soon as it was in the stored position, both Carly and Jodie saw it too. "I'll bet that is one of your grandfather's masterpieces," Jodie said to Vivian. "He worked the machine that designed the bottom covers."

Tim had caught on by now, too, and studied the wood cover.

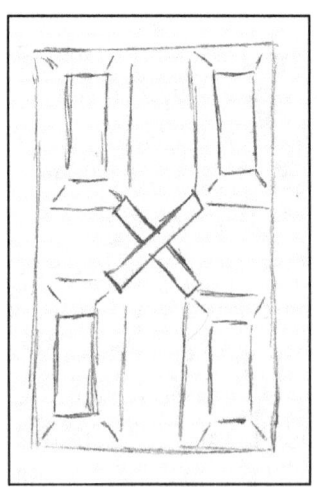

The Playhouse

"X marks the spot, right, Matey?" Tim's pirate accent was a bit off, but Gabby smiled back at his brother.

"Eagle River Detectives do not give up," Gabby said triumphantly, doing an arm pump.

"Remember how you told us Grandfather Grant found the undamaged Murphy bed in the room for misfit furniture and decided it would be perfect for the playhouse? Albert Decker was out of town that weekend and when he came back into work the next week, the bed was gone. I'm not sure if George knew about the bed, but he probably noticed when Albert checked on that room often, so he included it on the map. Albert probably blamed George for leading someone to the bed since there was no other way to explain the loss." Gabby had worked it all out shortly after seeing the bed.

Gramps walked over to the bed and made a close inspection of the wooden X in the center. "Right here I think." He pressed a small button on the side of the wood, causing the X to turn in a half circle revealing a cavity large enough to hold a notebook Albert had hidden there so long ago. *He probably learned about secret compartments from Gramps* was Gabby's guess. Gabby slid the treasure out of its hidey-hole and handed it to Ms. Sampson. "Here, I think this is what those men have been looking for."

Lila Sampson received the gift with reverence, shiny tears forming in her big brown eyes. "Thank you from the bottom of my heart." She looked at each of the kids. "Dad told me once what this meant to him. He did his experiments at a time when computers were slow to load and had unreliable connections in this part of the country.

He said he was working on a project with the government on harnessing hydroelectric power."

"You mean like those guys that are working on making cars run on water instead of gas?" Marco asked.

"He didn't give me the details, but he said he never recorded his discoveries anywhere but in his special notebooks, written by his own hand. He was devastated when he lost his notes. He made me promise if I ever found his notebook, that I would get it back in government hands as soon as possible. Now, thanks to the Eagle River Detectives, I can keep my promise to do just that," Lila said, thanking them all again.

"These kids are the real deal," said Ernie. Gramps was beaming proudly, and the look on Ernie's face was just as proud as Gramps'.

29

The Wrap-Up

The Eagle River Detectives sat at the picnic table in the backyard, still glowing with the satisfaction of a job well done. Gabby was the happiest of them all. He had doubted himself many times during the journey but had stuck it out anyway. Eagle River Detectives don't give up!

The sheriff had stopped by yesterday to inform them that the two men were indeed spies from a Middle Eastern country. Since that country depended on the sale of oil to fuel their economy, any new developments that would interfere with the world's dependence on oil, was a threat. Hydroelectric power might do that, so they had been tasked to find Albert Decker's notebook and destroy it. Thanks to the Eagle River Detectives, that notebook had been safely delivered into government hands, and the spies had been expelled from the country.

Gabby was happy to see them go. This whole thing started because he and Jodie were determined to get to the bottom of why their friends were being followed and harassed. Vivian had given Gabby a huge hug and Owen slapped his back in heartfelt appreciation for freeing them from what no kids should have to put up with. Mission accomplished!

The people at the factory were amused that the kids had tackled the treasure hunt that had begun so long ago and had found the treasure! George Evans was feeling a lot better about his crazy prank. He was grateful to learn that, in the end, it had led to the treasure. Lila Sampson had visited him at Sumner Place and told him how pleased her father would have been with the way things turned out.

Tonight's meeting had only one thing on the agenda. Marco sat at the table, eyes wide, soaking up all the talk and kidding going on with the group. He had been officially welcomed into The Eagle River Detectives club, and tonight was his first meeting. Gabby was pleased to have this sharp kid on the team. "So, what do you think, Marco?" he asked the new detective.

"This is awesome!" said Marco.

THE END

Author's Note

I originally wrote this series for 9 to 17-year-olds but found that my senior friends enjoyed the story as much as the kids, so now I think of it as a Cozy Mystery "Lite."

Thank you for reading my book. If you liked it, I would love to read your review on Amazon.

This book has a free collection of activity sheets. To get the FREE activity booklet end an email to: katherineklemp@gmail.com or sign up at: www.katherineklemp.com and use the drop-down menu to find your bundle.

About the Author

Katherine H. Klemp is the mother of eight children. Her kids, as children, were lively, smart, and crazy—a lot like the Grant kids in this adventure. (They haven't changed and have taught their children to be just like them!) The family sang together and toured around the country in a big blue bus for three weeks every summer, singing at churches and festivals. Katherine is a retired registered nurse currently living in White Bear Township, MN.

www.ingramcontent.com/pod-product-compliance
Lightning Source LLC
LaVergne TN
LVHW010216070526
838199LV00062B/4612